TANGLEWOOD ANIMAL PARK

The Troublesome Tiger

Zoe couldn't help exchanging a worried look with Oliver. She really hoped she could find something that Tindu the tiger loved – she hated seeing him so unhappy. If Tindu couldn't be tempted out of his pen, it might even mean that they would have to find him a new home. And without Tindu, there'd be no reason to bring in Koko, the female tiger. Tanglewood might end up with no terrific tigers at all!

For Taz, my very own tiny Tindu.

First published in the UK in 2017 by Usborne Publishing Ltd.,
Usborne House, 83-85 Saffron Hill, London EC1N 8RT, England.
www.usborne.com

Copyright © Tamsyn Murray, 2017

The right of Tamsyn Murray to be identified as the author
of this work has been asserted by her in accordance with the
Copyright, Designs and Patents Act, 1988.

Cover and inside illustrations by Chuck Groenink.
Inside illustrations by Jean Claude, Courtesy of Advocate Art.
Illustrations copyright © Usborne Publishing Ltd., 2017

The name Usborne and the devices 🎈 🌐 are Trade Marks of
Usborne Publishing Ltd.

A CIP catalogue record for this book is available from the British Library.

This edition published in America in 2017 AE.

PB ISBN 9780794540470   ALB ISBN 9781601304285

J MAMJJASOND/18 03899/5
Printed in China.

Chapter One

"Is he here?"

Zoe Fox closed the front door of Tanglewood Manor and waited.

The warm September sun poured through the criss-cross leaded windows. There was no answer.

Breathless with excitement, she dumped her school bag in the grand, wooden-paneled hall and hurried straight into the kitchen in search of her mother. Normally, the first thing Zoe did when she got home from school was dash up the sweeping staircase to her room, to trade her sticky uniform for shorts and a Team Tanglewood polo shirt. Then she'd head into the animal park that surrounded her home and wander from enclosure to enclosure, saying hello to her favorite furry friends. But today was different. Today, she was desperate to hear about their newest arrival: Tindu the tiger, who was coming from a zoo on the other side of the country.

"Mom," she said, skidding to a halt in front of the kitchen table. "Is Tindu here?"

Mrs. Fox smiled as she looked up from the animal book she was reading with Rory, Zoe's four-year-old little brother. "Yes, he's here."

Zoe felt a thrill of excitement wiggle through her. She'd seen Sumatran tigers at other zoos and she couldn't wait to meet Tindu.

"Don't get too excited," Mom went on. "We need to have a little chat before you go racing off."

There was a guarded note in her voice that made Zoe's heart sink. She'd been distracted at school all day, wondering whether the tiger had arrived safely or whether he'd been held up on his way to Tanglewood. Transporting any animal could be tricky – they had no way of understanding what was happening, or why, and could easily get upset – but Zoe knew both her parents had been especially worried about Tindu's move. Sumatran tigers were critically endangered, hunted by poachers and chased from their homes by humans; every single animal was important to make sure the species survived. It was vital that Tindu arrived at Tanglewood happy and healthy, ready to get to know his new home.

"Is everything okay?" she asked, trying to squash a sudden burst of worry.

Mom gave her a sympathetic look. "He's fine. But you can't see him – not yet. Dad and the big cat

🐾 5 🐾

keepers want to keep the area around his enclosure as quiet as possible."

Zoe nodded, trying to hide her disappointment. She knew how important it was for Tindu to get used to his brand-new, eco-friendly enclosure without too many distractions, so that he wasn't frightened or nervous. Then, once everyone was sure he'd settled in, her parents and the Tanglewood keepers would introduce him to Koko, a female tiger who was due to move from another zoo. If everything went well, they planned to hold a Terrific Tigers weekend in October to help raise awareness of the dangers faced by all tigers. Tindu and Koko would be the star attractions.

But that wasn't the only reason Zoe's parents were hoping Tindu would settle into his new home fast. With only four hundred Sumatran tigers in the wild, it was more important than ever to make sure there were plenty in zoos around the world. Wild tigers might prefer to live on their own, but in zoos they were often kept in pairs or trios. There wasn't room to give each one an enclosure of their own, and having another tiger around helped to make zoo life more fun. And if Tindu and Koko liked each other enough, there might even be the pitter-patter of tiny tiger paws around Tanglewood in the future. Zoe couldn't think of anything cuter. Ever since she'd been lucky enough to see the birth of baby zebra Flash at Tanglewood, she'd been hoping for more zoo-borns. Little tiger cubs would be amazing…

"How was Tindu's journey?" Zoe asked.

"Okay, I think," Mom said. "He's a little tired and confused, as you'd expect. He has no idea what's happening, after all. It must be scary for him."

Zoe thought back to when her family had moved to Tanglewood in the summer; she'd been excited but a little bit nervous too, even though *she'd* known what was happening.

Tindu had been shut inside a crate during his move, unable to see what was going on; although he'd been perfectly safe, Zoe could understand why he'd be upset.

Mom seemed to sense she was disappointed.

"There's an observation camera in Tindu's den. Why don't you run over to the control room and watch the live feed from there?"

Zoe felt her spirits lift a little. She might not be able to see Tindu in the fur but a video stream in Tanglewood HQ was the next best thing. Grabbing a bag of chips from the pantry, she dashed out of the kitchen. "Thanks, Mom!"

Tanglewood HQ was in another wing of the old manor house, away from the part Zoe and her family lived in. It was the control room for the park's security team. All the video feeds from the cameras around the zoo were shown on a wall of screens. It was like watching lots of televisions at once. Zoe had spent several fascinated hours there, watching the action around the zoo and chatting with the different security guards. They didn't know as much about animals as the keepers, but they spent so much time keeping an eye on things that Zoe found they were full of interesting stories.

She tapped on the door and waited for it to open.

To her surprise, the lemur keeper, Mizbah, let her in. It wasn't unusual to find a keeper inside Tanglewood HQ – they often observed their animals from a distance – but Mizbah usually liked to be out in the park, being hands-on with her lemurs. Zoe didn't blame her; the ring-tailed lemurs were her absolute favorite animals too. She'd hang out with them every day if she had the chance.

"Hi, Zoe," Mizbah said, smiling. "I bet you've come to spy on our latest arrival as well."

Mizbah was curious about Tindu too, Zoe realized with a grin.

"That's right," she said, waving to the security guard. "Hey, Hans."

Hans waved back. "Good afternoon, Zoe. I think you want screen six."

Zoe gazed at the panel of screens until she found the right one, trained on the tiger den. "Have you been watching long? How is Tindu doing?"

"I finished my shift about half an hour ago and have been here ever since," Mizbah said, sighing.

"Poor Tindu, he's not very happy. In fact, he's still inside his crate at the moment."

She pointed at the corner of the screen. The camera was focused on the tiger's den – a wide concrete room, split into three living spaces by metal bars. The spaces were connected by hatches, which could be opened or closed, and each one also had a low door leading to the outside habitat so that the tigers could choose whether they were inside or out. The den had a public viewing area, although visitors were separated from the tigers by two sets of bars and a large gap. Only keepers were allowed to stand in the gap between the bars, and it was absolutely forbidden for anyone to go inside the den with a tiger. Strict rules were in place to make sure everyone stayed safe.

One of the spaces had a large pile of straw in the corner – Zoe guessed that was for sleeping – and what looked like a tasty meat treat nearby. At the edge of the picture, outside the bars, Zoe could just make out the shadow of a person – her dad, maybe, or Cassie, the senior big-cat keeper. There was no sign of Tindu, though. None at all.

Mizbah pointed at the furthest den wall.

"He's in there, hiding in the crate on the other side of that hatch," she said. "Eventually, he'll get hungry and come out."

He probably feels safe in the crate, Zoe thought. She knew his previous keepers at his last zoo had spent a long time making sure he was comfortable in it ahead of his long journey to Tanglewood. She also knew that a scared, unsure tiger was a dangerous one – another reason Zoe hoped he'd traveled well. She hated the thought of any animal being unhappy.

"What if he doesn't come out?" Zoe asked, her voice small. "What if he stays in there or doesn't like it here?"

"Let's give him a chance," Mizbah said. "He's only been here a few hours after all."

They watched for a while as shadows flitted around the edge of the screen but there was no sign of Tindu.

"Why not come back in the morning?" Mizbah suggested. "He might be feeling braver by then."

Reluctantly, Zoe agreed. She knew it would take time for Tindu to get used to his new surroundings, but she'd hoped to catch a glimpse of him at least. Sighing, she said goodbye to Mizbah and Hans and made her way upstairs to change out of her school uniform.

Zoe decided that she'd go and visit Flash once she'd changed. The zebra foal was so cute it was impossible to feel anything other than happy around him. She'd caught the bus home from school with Oliver and he'd mentioned he'd be there. As the son of Tanglewood's Chief Vet he had responsibilities around the park, just like Zoe, and one of his jobs was to help look after the zebras. Maybe Zoe would be able to give him a hand.

Oliver lived in one of Tanglewood Manor's side cottages. He and Zoe had just started at the same school too, although they were in different classes. *He's almost as animal-crazy as I am*, Zoe thought. *I bet he's itching to find out what's happening with Tindu too.*

Zoe felt better as soon she walked into the park. It was almost closing time – any visiting schoolchildren were long gone and there was a sense of calm that Zoe knew wouldn't be there on the weekend. She loved seeing the park full of visitors, peering in at the animals with happy, amazed faces, but she liked it more once the gates had closed and she had Tanglewood almost to herself.

A loud roar shattered the peace, rumbling over the park like ferocious thunder. Zoe grinned – that would be Sinbad, Tanglewood's majestic African lion. He lived with four females over at Big Cat Mountain and he loved letting everyone know who was boss. His roar carried for miles – sometimes, it was the first thing Zoe heard when she woke up. Now he was probably hungry – the big-cat keepers would be preparing the lions' feed and it sounded as though Sinbad couldn't wait.

Zoe took the long way around to the zebra field, circling up past the red pandas to loop under the high wooden walkways of Snowy Point. This was where Tanglewood's snow leopards lived in the amazing enclosure Zoe's mom had designed for them. Zoe paused for a moment to watch Minty and Tara as they padded along the logs that hung from the ceiling, admiring their silvery gray fur. Dragging herself away, she headed once more for the zebras.

There was still a small crowd gathered there and Zoe soon understood why – Flash was going for cute overload. He was frisking all over the field, tossing his stubby black mane and kicking up his heels while his mother, Candy, looked on.

"He's so adorable," one woman said, snapping photo after photo on her phone.

A little girl with her face painted like a butterfly tugged on the woman's hand. "Can we get a baby zebra, Mommy? Please?"

Zoe leaned on the fence, grinning. She remembered asking her own mother almost exactly the same question when she was four, except she'd wanted to take an elephant home with her.

"I don't think a zebra would get along with our rabbit," the woman said. "And I think they might bite."

Flash looked up and saw Zoe. He came trotting over, whinnying in hello, and she reached over the fence to gently pat his neck.

"That girl is touching him!" the child said, her eyes widening.

"That's because I work here and Flash knows me," Zoe explained. "Zebras can bite and kick, especially if they're scared."

Flash nuzzled at her pockets, his black-tipped ears flicking back and forth as he looked for treats. It was difficult to imagine a less dangerous-looking animal, Zoe thought with a smile, but they could really fight back when they felt threatened. Luckily, the Tanglewood zebras were fairly tame.

"See?" the woman said, flashing Zoe a grateful smile. "We can't have a pet zebra, no matter how cute they are. Now come on, you. Time to go home."

They walked away, just as Jenna the zebra keeper arrived, with Oliver behind her.

"Hi, Zoe," she said. "Want to help us with the grooming?"

Zoe smiled. "I was hoping you'd say that."

Oliver handed her a wooden dandy brush. "The more the merrier," he said with a grin. "Grooming makes my arms ache after a while."

Jenna pulled a bunch of keys from her pocket and undid the padlock and the safety lock on the gate of the enclosure. Zoe followed her inside and Flash came trotting towards her.

"I don't have any snacks for you today," she told the zebra foal, laughing. "Sorry."

Oliver held up a carrot. "Look what I brought. But you can't have it until later."

Zoe and Oliver got to work brushing the dust from the black-and-white striped coats. Most of the zebras stood patiently while they were being groomed, making gentle nicker sounds as their stripes began to shine. It was amazing to think that each pattern was unique. Tanglewood had eight zebras in total and the keepers had kept Candy and Flash separate from the other zebras when he was first born, partly to make sure Flash was safe but also to give him time to learn and recognize his mother's stripes. Zebras might look the same to the untrained eye but their patterns were just like fingerprints.

Once the grooming was done and the stalls were cleaned out, Zoe and Oliver said goodbye to Jenna and walked back towards the manor house. Tall wooden fences hid the tiger enclosure from view as they passed. Zoe's mother had spent weeks working on the new habitat, ready for Tindu to move in. It used the same eco-friendly materials and techniques as Snowy Point, harvesting rainwater from the roof to water the plants inside and top up the waterfall. There was even a swimming pool, with heated rocks dotted around so that Tindu could keep warm in the colder months, and plenty of places for Tanglewood's visitors to admire him from behind the toughened safety glass windows. *All we need now is for Tindu to*

Zoe nodded. "Exactly – so where has it come from?"

"Maybe it's a stray," he suggested. "Or a feral cat – you know, a wild one."

Zoe felt her heart sink a little. If it was a stray then that meant someone was missing it. It was probably hungry too. She took a few steps towards it, holding out one hand. "Here, kitty. Are you friendly?"

The cat turned tail and ran.

"I guess that answers your question," Oliver said, starting to walk across the grass towards his own home. "See you tomorrow."

Zoe stared at the trees where the orange tabby had vanished.

"Yeah, see you," she said in a distracted tone.

"Don't worry," he called. "It'll probably have found its way home by the morning."

But Zoe *was* worried. She couldn't just pretend she hadn't seen the cat – what if it was lost, far from home and all alone in the woods? Thinking fast, she hurried into the house and opened up a can of tuna.

She spooned some onto an old plate and left it outside the back door. There was every chance the fish would be gone by the morning, eaten by a passing fox from the woods, but it made her feel a little bit better to think that maybe the orange tabby might find it first.

"Be lucky, kitty," she whispered, as she closed the back door.

Chapter Two

At first, Zoe was confused when her alarm went off early on Saturday morning. *It's the weekend*, she thought groggily, wondering why she'd set it at all. Then she remembered: Tindu was here! She bounced out of bed and got dressed in a hurry.

In the kitchen, Rory tried to get her to help him with his puzzle.

"Maybe later," she told him.

"Would you like some cereal?" Mom asked,

reaching into one of the cabinets for a bowl.

"No time for breakfast," Zoe replied.

She grabbed an apple from the fruit bowl on the table and hurried along to Tanglewood HQ.

This time, Ruth was the security guard on duty. She smiled when she saw Zoe.

"Hans said he thought you'd stop by this morning," she said, letting Zoe in. "Have you come to check out the tiger?"

Zoe nodded, her eyes scanning the screens. But there was no sign of Tindu. The meat the keepers had left out for him had vanished, but she didn't know if he had taken it to eat in the night or whether it had been removed to stop the flies from landing on it.

She turned to Ruth. "Have you seen him at all?"

The security guard yawned. "Not yet, and I've been here since six o'clock. He's a shy one."

Zoe swallowed her disappointment and watched the screen, hoping for a glimpse of orange-and-black fur, but Tindu was staying well hidden.

"Did he eat the food the keepers left out," she asked Ruth.

Ruth shook her head. "No. The keepers cleared it away earlier."

Zoe sighed. Food could often tempt the most timid of animals, but it seemed as though Tindu wasn't interested. Another thirty minutes went by with no sign of Tindu. Zoe and Ruth chatted about the other animals they saw on the screens but eventually Zoe had to give up. She said goodbye and headed back to the kitchen.

Rory and Mom were sitting at the table surrounded by cardboard boxes, torn-up strips of newspaper and a lot of straw. The air was filled with the scent of lemons, and there was a bowl of chopped up apples and grapes nearby.

"Look what we've been up to," Mom said, waving an empty toilet paper roll at her.

Zoe poked her head out of the kitchen door to check the plate: empty, just as she'd expected, with no sign of the orange tabby or any other animal.

She closed the door and turned back to Rory and Mom.

"Hmmm," she said, frowning, as she stared at the cluttered table. "Let me guess..."

Rory bounced up and down on his chair, eyes shining, obviously desperate to explain.

Zoe smiled. "I give in. What are you doing?"

"We're making meerkat treats," he explained. "So they don't get bored."

Zoe nodded. Playtime and toys were important for all animals raised in captivity, to give them little challenges and to remind them of their wild side every now and then. And Zoe's mom was an animal habitat designer, so she was great at finding ways to improve the meerkats' lives.

"So you're stuffing the boxes with straw and paper and chopped-up fruit for the meerkats to explore," Zoe said, wrinkling her nose. "What are the lemons for?"

"To rub over the outside of the boxes," Mom said. "We want to stimulate their sense of smell too."

"Mom's got a box of bugs," Rory told Zoe, pointing to a clear plastic box filled with a variety of different insects. "We're going to let the meerkats catch them."

Zoe grimaced. She liked all the animals at Tanglewood but she had to admit that insects weren't her favorites.

"We thought you might like to help," Mom said. "Once we've finished filling these boxes we can head over to the meerkat house and give them these for breakfast."

Zoe sat down at the table and picked up an empty tube. "Sounds like fun."

The boxes and tubes were filled in no time, with chunks of apples and grapes hidden inside. Zoe, Rory and Mom gathered them all up and set off for the meerkat enclosure.

"I'll message Oliver and tell him to meet us there," Zoe said as they walked through the gate between the manor house and the park. "He'd love to help with this."

The meerkat enclosure had been given a makeover

before the grand Tanglewood reopening. A path led between two sandy, glass-sided pits, with meerkats in each. Overhead, there was a narrow see-through tunnel across the path so that the meerkats could travel between the two enclosures – Rory loved to stand underneath and watch the meerkats scurry back and forth. One enclosure had a golden-brown mound for the meerkat on guard duty to keep watch from, and the other had a snug den, complete with heat lamps, for the others to retreat to when the weather turned chilly.

"Look, there's Jack," Zoe called, spotting one of the meerkat keepers by the entrance to the enclosure.

Rory pointed along the path. "And there's Oliver."

Jack raised an eyebrow when he saw all the boxes. "Wow, these guys are in for a real treat."

Mrs. Fox held up her container of spindly-legged insects. "We brought some of these too. Nothing but the best for our animals."

Oliver cleared his throat. "In the wild, meerkats eat all kinds of insects, even scorpions and spiders.

They're from the mongoose family, which makes them immune to some kinds of venom."

Zoe hid a smile – Oliver never missed an opportunity to show off his animal knowledge.

"They're too smart to eat the scorpion's stinger, though," she said. "They bite it off, then use sand to rub off any traces of poison on the scorpion's body before they eat it, just in case!"

Jack looked impressed. "Gold stars for both of you. Meerkats even teach their young how to prepare a scorpion for eating." He smiled at Rory, whose eyes had grown wide. "I suppose it's a little like showing you how to peel an orange before you eat it."

"Except an orange doesn't try to kill you," Zoe said, making a face. "Don't worry, Rory, there are no scorpions in Mom's box."

"Just crickets and grasshoppers." Mom smiled. "Should we go inside?"

Jack opened the padlocks on the gates. There were ten golden-brown meerkats in total, with long, inquisitive noses and dark-ringed eyes. No sooner had Zoe sat down than the meerkats scampered over to her, pulling the lids off the boxes and poking their long slender fingers inside the cardboard tubes in search of fruit. Mrs. Fox removed the lid of the insect box and planted it upside down on the sandy floor, trapping the crickets. The meerkats leaped at it, digging underneath the edges to get to the snacks inside.

"Careful!" Zoe said, laughing as one of the meerkats scrambled across her lap to pounce on a cricket. "There's plenty for everyone."

One of the younger meerkats decided Oliver's shoulder was the best place to eat his snack, which Rory found hilarious. Another pair fought so hard over a cricket that it hopped away and they both squeaked in dismay when they realized. The fun went on for another ten minutes, until the boxes were empty and all the treats had been gobbled up. Then the meerkats began to play with each other, wrestling and racing around the enclosure.

Zoe checked her watch. "Yikes, it's not long until

opening time," she said, jumping to her feet. "I need to get over to Guinea Pig Central! It's my turn to clean out the guinea pigs this morning."

"Want some help?" Oliver said.

Zoe flashed him a grateful smile. Sometimes it was hard to believe they'd ever been enemies. "Okay, I'll race you from the gate," she said, dusting the sand from her legs. "Last one there is a dung beetle."

"Have fun," Mom called, as she, Rory and Jack began to clean up what was left of the meerkats' playtime.

Taking care not to disturb the animals, Zoe crossed to the gate. Oliver arrived at the same time and they jostled, although Zoe saw he took just as much care as she did to ensure the gate was properly closed before they raced off along the path. Zoe was half tempted to slow down and peer into the tiger house for a sneaky glimpse of Tindu, but the doors were firmly closed and she didn't dare try to open them. As frustrating as it was, she'd simply have to wait until later to find out how the tiger was doing.

Oliver veered right to go past Snowy Point, while Zoe doubled back past Wolf Woods. As she rounded the corner, she saw the ring-tailed lemurs had just been fed too. They were munching on slices of melon and sweet potato, their black-and-white tails waving happily. Zoe slowed to a halt and watched in fascination as their thin gray fingers picked and chose from the food.

Suddenly, the leader of the group, Bindi, stopped eating and turned her amber eyes sharply towards the sky. The others quickly copied her, staring upwards like peculiar little statues. Zoe squinted at the sky and saw a plane in the distance, skimming the clouds.

"Don't worry, it's not a bird," she said, laughing. "A plane won't steal your melon, Bindi."

She said goodbye to the lemurs and walked the rest of the way to the guinea-pig enclosure. Oliver was waiting, looking triumphant. "I won," he said. "Looks like you're the dung beetle!"

Zoe smiled. Dung beetles were strong and they

liked to clean up after other animals.

"Then I'm in exactly the right place," she told Oliver. "Have you seen how much guinea pigs poop?"

Not that Zoe minded that – the guinea pigs were among her favorite animals at Tanglewood. She loved how soft their fur was, the friendly way they tumbled over each other to say hello when they thought she might have a snack, and the cute meeping sound they made almost all the time. And she loved being able to get close to them – it was almost like having a pet.

With Oliver to help, the cleaning up didn't take long. They'd both been around animals enough to know exactly what needed to be done, and they made a good team. Zoe was just placing the last guinea pig onto the fresh sawdust inside the pen when she paused and frowned.

"Look at this, Oliver," she said, running her fingers over a small bald patch on the back of the little creature's fluffy black neck. "Zak's lost some fur."

Oliver picked his way carefully across the pen

and peered at the guinea pig. "Yeah, he has. Have they been treated for fleas recently?"

"I'm sure they have," Zoe said, her frown deepening. "Paolo is really good at keeping on top of things like that. Your dad is too."

Oliver rubbed his chin thoughtfully. "True. Maybe it's an allergy?"

Zoe held Zak up to get a good look at his face. "His eyes aren't watery, though." She lowered the guinea pig to the floor. "I'll mention it to Paolo, see what he says."

Once the guinea-pig pen was locked, Oliver and Zoe started to walk back to the manor house.

"I think Dad's a little worried about Tindu," Oliver admitted as they walked. "He's still not eating."

"I know," Zoe said. "Everyone is – but it's only been one day. Tigers can go for several days without food – I bet he'll come out when he's hungry."

Oliver kicked at a stone on the path. "But it's the Terrific Tigers weekend two weeks from today.

What if Tindu doesn't settle down at all?"

Zoe had thought exactly the same thing, but she didn't tell Oliver that. Instead, she did her best to sound reassuring. "Tindu isn't the first troublesome tiger Dad's had to deal with. I bet your dad has dealt with a few too, and the keepers here are great. They'll figure it out."

Oliver nodded. "I know Suki isn't a tiger but it took her ages to settle in when she first came here," he said. "I don't suppose lions are that different from tigers when it comes to new homes."

"But she had Sinbad and the other lions to make friends with," Zoe pointed out. "I bet that helped. Tindu lived with other tigers at his old zoo – he doesn't have anyone here."

"Maybe he's lonely," Oliver said. "But the sooner he gets comfortable, the sooner Koko can arrive and make friends."

If only we could make Tindu understand how exciting life at Tanglewood is going to be, Zoe thought to herself as they crunched across the gravel towards the manor. *What if he was afraid?* she wondered. She thought of the meerkats, with one of them always keeping watch, and the lemurs scanning the sky for predators. In the wild, animals survived on their instincts – she supposed those instincts were hard to ignore, even when there was no real danger.

"The meerkats were funny," Oliver said, cutting into her thoughts. "I thought they were going to start eating those cardboard boxes!"

Zoe smiled absently, her mind still on Tindu. "Well, we did rub the outside with lemon juice so that they smelled zingy."

"They were definitely interested," Oliver said. "I'm pretty sure one of them was drooling."

Zoe laughed then. "I guess they *really* like the smell of lemons."

Oliver's eyes lit up. "Hey, we should try something like that with Tindu," he said. "Big cats use their sense of smell to stalk and chase their prey."

Zoe tilted her head. "We could put something irresistible outside his den, to tempt him out." An idea popped into her head. "Or we could lay a scent trail for him to follow."

"That's a good idea – and it could work," Oliver said.

"Let's make a list of smells he might like," Zoe suggested, feeling a little burst of enthusiasm at the thought of doing something to help Tindu. "Then we can see which ones will work the best."

Oliver grimaced. "I promised Dad I'd clean my room today. Can you start us off?"

"Sure," Zoe said. "I can fill you in."

He nodded. "See you later then," he said, and headed home.

Zoe went into the manor, gnawing on her lip as she walked. There had to be something Tindu would find irresistible. But what could it be?

Chapter Three

After lunch, Zoe settled down at the kitchen table with her tablet, searching for ideas to help Tindu feel more at home. Rory sat next to her, interested at first, and tried to help, but he soon became bored.

"You said you would help me with my puzzle," he said in a grumpy voice, when Zoe pushed his hands off the screen for the fourth time.

"Not now," Zoe said in a faraway voice as she scanned an article about a tiger's sense of smell.

They didn't like lemon or citrus scents much but it seemed that they did like some spices.

"You said you would," Rory insisted, and now he sounded tearful rather than grumpy.

Mom looked up from her work.

"You did say that, Zoe." She glanced out of the window. "It's a nice afternoon. Why don't you take him for a ride on the train instead?"

Zoe swallowed a sigh of frustration – what she really wanted was to build up her list to share with Oliver. But then she caught sight of Rory's unhappy expression and changed her mind. She might have an idea while she was out, and the little train that chugged its way around Tanglewood was fun.

"Okay," she said, ruffling her little brother's hair. "Come on."

The train wasn't busy. During the summer, the line to ride it had stretched a long way back from the white picket fence beside the pretend station, and there had been two engines chugging around the track all day. But Zoe knew they'd timed things well; a lot of Tanglewood's visitors would be listening to the Birds of Prey talk down at the aviary, or watching the penguins being fed.

"Where to, Zoe?" Pete the train driver asked as they sat down in one of the brightly painted cars.

Zoe grinned as she pretended to consider the question. The train only ever went one way but it was fun to act as though they had a choice. "I don't know. What do you think, Rory?"

"Africa," he said immediately. "I want to see the gazelles."

Pete rang the bell and fired up the engine. "Next stop, the Serengeti!"

The train lurched forwards and sure enough Zoe soon saw the gazelles grazing inside their enclosure, the thick black stripe on their sides stark against the rest of their pale-brown hide. Some raised their heads, their long thin horns pointing to the sky, as the train went by, but most ignored it completely. Next, they passed the spotted hyenas. Rory wasn't as in to them as the graceful gazelles but Zoe loved to hear them whoop and giggle. And then they came to a wide, fenced-off area that was being developed to create a new attraction – the Serengeti Safari, which would be a number of new enclosures that visitors could only reach aboard the Safari Express Train. *One day soon we'll have giraffes and elephants there,* Zoe thought, her tummy fluttering with anticipation. She couldn't wait!

The train chugged on, looping around the back of Wolf Woods. As the engine pulled up to the platform, Zoe's phone vibrated with a message from Oliver.

Dad loves the scent idea! He wants you to come to meet us at the tiger house in fifteen minutes.

Zoe felt a thrill of excitement: did that mean she was about to meet Tindu? She thanked Pete for the ride and helped Rory climb out of the little car – if she hurried, she might just get him home before it was time to meet Oliver and Max...

"Again!" Rory said, tugging on her hand.

"I don't think so," she said gently. "I need to go and see Tindu now."

Rory's eyes lit up. "I want to come."

Zoe sighed. "Sorry, Rory, not this time. Tindu needs peace and quiet and you're not that good at being quiet."

Her little brother frowned. "Sometimes I am." He squinted and lowered his voice to a whisper. "See? This is me being quiet."

It was true, Zoe thought. Rory *could* be silent and calm. But like most four-year-olds, he didn't stay that way for long.

"No," she said. "I'm taking you back to Mom."

Rory complained all the way back to the manor, although Zoe did her best to distract him with a game of I-Spy.

"Cloud," he guessed, peering up at the sky.

"No."

"Cobra."

Zoe looked around. "Where?"

Her brother shrugged. "In the reptile house."

"It doesn't count if you can't see it right now," she reminded him, grinning. "Guess again."

Rory was quiet until they rounded the corner of the house. "Cat!"

"What?" Zoe said, her head whipping around. "Where?"

Rory pointed to the trees. "Over there. But it ran away when it saw us."

Zoe hesitated. It couldn't be a coincidence – there couldn't be *two* mystery cats hanging around the yard, could there? "Where, Rory?" she asked. "Show me." She was about to go and look when her phone vibrated with another message from Oliver.

I'm here. Where are you?

The cat would have to wait for now. Zoe hurried towards the front door. "Come on, Rory, let's get you inside," she said.

It was Tindu time!

There was a familiar crowd at the entrance to the

tiger enclosure. Zoe's dad was there, with Oliver and Max, along with Cassie, the senior big-cat keeper. They all looked up as Zoe approached.

"Good, you're here," Mr. Fox said briskly. He glanced at Zoe and Oliver. "Now, I'm sure I don't have to remind you both that Tindu is still a long way from being comfortable with us yet, so you'll have to be very quiet and stand back, with no sudden movements or noises."

Zoe and Oliver exchanged a look. They'd been told exactly the same thing when Candy the zebra had been about to give birth to Flash, and Zoe felt the same surge of excitement.

"Got it," she said, nodding.

"Of course," Oliver said. "We'll be quiet."

Mr. Fox looked satisfied. "Okay, ready when you are, Cassie."

"Thanks," Cassie said. "The good news is that Tindu is out of his crate now, as you'll see. But he's very jittery and shows no sign of wanting to explore yet."

Zoe frowned. It was unusual for a tiger not to want to check out a new territory – Tindu must be very nervous. She thought of the food she'd spotted in the den the night before. "Has he eaten anything?"

Cassie shook her head. "No. We've tried leaving food out but he didn't even sniff it. I'm not too concerned about that for now – in the wild, he might easily go a few days without feeding and he only ate every three days at his old zoo anyway." She pulled open the door. "Should we go in?"

Zoe held her breath as she went inside the tiger house. It was her first visit since her mother had redesigned it and she couldn't wait to see all the clever, thoughtful touches her mom had put in place both there, and in the outside enclosure, to make Tindu comfortable. Inside, it looked just as she'd seen on the screen at Tanglewood HQ; there were two fences – an outer one, made of widely spaced metal bars, and an inner one made of thick wire. In between the two there was a space wide enough for a keeper to stand. Beyond the inner fence, Zoe saw three dens, separated by wire fences. The left and the middle ones were empty. But the right-hand side was not. Her heart thudded in excitement: lying on an untidy rectangle of straw was a magnificent flame-orange tiger.

Tindu lay with his head resting on his paws, his amber eyes fixed on the intruders. His black-striped tail flicked back and forth as he bared his teeth in a low rumbling snarl. Zoe caught sight of two long white fangs beneath his quivering whiskers and his ears were flattened against his head. He did not look happy.

"Hello, Tindu," Cassie said in a calm but cheerful voice. "Enough of the grumpiness. I've brought you some fresh meat."

For one wild moment, Zoe thought the big-cat keeper meant her and Oliver! Then she noticed the wide tool belt Cassie wore around her waist; it had a cup holder that was filled with cubes of raw meat. That must be Tindu's treat.

"The trick is to get him to trust us," Cassie said to

Zoe and Oliver. "And the quickest way to an animal's heart is through its stomach."

Cassie unlocked the gate in the outer fence and slipped through to stand in the gap between the fences. "If we can form a bond with Tindu it will help him to settle in. Then he might feel safe enough to explore the rest of his new home," she said.

Zoe glanced at the corner of the den and saw that the hatch that led to the outside habitat was open. It was attached to a pulley system so that it could be safely controlled by the keeper. But Tindu showed no interest in leaving his den – he stayed on the straw, watching them with distrustful eyes.

He really was a beauty, Zoe thought, despite his grumpiness. His orange and black stripes were sleek and glossy until they reached his neck, where they expanded into a magnificent white, orange and black ruff. He'd be a huge star at Tanglewood...if they could persuade him to trust his new keepers.

Cassie took a small cube of meat between her gloved fingers and bent low to push it through a gap in the inner fence. Instantly, Tindu's gaze shifted. His nostrils flared as he sniffed the air. His mouth opened as the scent reached him. Zoe tensed. He must be hungry. But would it be enough to overcome his caution?

"Come on," Oliver muttered, almost too quiet to hear. "Try it."

The straw rustled as the tiger shifted his weight and he bared his teeth in another long, rumbling growl. Cassie wiggled her fingers, making the meat dance. Zoe bit her lip, willing the big cat to take the treat. But just as she was certain he would get up to investigate, Tindu turned his head away.

Cassie sighed. "We've tried meat, fish, even ice cubes made from frozen blood," she said, withdrawing her hand, "but he's not interested yet."

"Give it time," Mr. Fox advised. "It's early days, anyway. I'm sure he'll come around soon."

"Oliver and Zoe had a good idea," Max said. "They wondered if there was a particular scent Tindu might find irresistible."

"We thought maybe you could lay a scent trail," Oliver said. "Zoe was researching ideas for smells."

Cassie turned an interested gaze on Zoe and Oliver. "That *is* a good idea. What did you come up with?"

Zoe opened up the list she'd made on her tablet. "There were some obvious things, like fish and meat. And the experts mentioned some rich spices like cinnamon and ginger." She shook her head in amazement. "I'm not sure how good that idea is, though."

"It's a great idea," Cassie said, smiling. "Let me do some research of my own and we'll see what might work with Tindu."

Zoe was happy that Cassie loved the idea of a scent trail, but she couldn't help exchanging a worried look with Oliver. She really hoped she could find something that Tindu loved – she hated seeing him so unhappy. If Tindu couldn't be tempted out of his pen, it might even mean that they would have to find him a new home. And without Tindu,

Chapter Four

"Any news?" Oliver asked.

It was Monday afternoon and the school bus was trundling towards Tanglewood. Zoe was checking her phone for messages.

"Nothing new," she sighed. "Tindu still won't come out of the den. He's pacing around so much that Cassie and your dad are worrying about the pads on his paws."

Oliver shook his head. "I know the den floor

needs to be concrete, but I wish we could put down a carpet or something."

Zoe made a face. The problem was that tiger urine was very strong – so strong that it ate through anything except concrete. "Can you imagine the smell?"

Now it was Oliver's turn to grimace. "Yuck – I'd rather not."

"At least they've managed to move him into the den next door to his, so he isn't sleeping on dirty straw," Zoe said. "But he still won't eat."

"He will," Oliver said. "He just needs to learn to trust us, that's all."

As soon as they got home, Zoe dashed to the guinea pigs, hoping to get the pen cleaned out in record time so that she could check in with Cassie and Tindu. But when she arrived at Guinea Pig Central, Paolo the guinea-pig keeper was already there, standing in the center of the enclosure.

Zoe stared at him in confusion. "Oh! I was sure it was my turn today. Did I get it wrong?"

Paolo smiled. "No, you're not wrong. A few of our little furry friends need to move house, that's all." He bent down and gathered up one of the guinea pigs. "Including Zak here. Want to help?"

"Sure," Zoe said, rolling up her sleeves. A flutter of uneasiness started in her stomach. "But why are they moving?"

"You remember Zak lost a big clump of fur last week?" Paolo said, reaching down to pick up a small, black-haired guinea pig.

"Of course," Zoe replied, remembering how she'd noticed the animal's bald patch and brought it to the keeper's attention. "You thought he'd had a fight with one of the other guinea pigs."

"That's right. He's lost a lot more fur today," Paolo said, turning the animal around to show Zoe several patches of pale-pink skin along his side and neck. "And if you look closely, you'll see a couple of marks that look a lot like they were made with teeth."

"Oh no!" Zoe said, with a rush of sympathy for Zak. "So he *is* fighting?"

"Not quite," Paolo said. He put the little creature into a pet carrier and reached for another animal. "It's something called 'barbering', where one guinea pig chews another's fur. It's quite common and doesn't always cause a problem but in poor Zak's case, I think he's being singled out."

He pointed to another guinea pig, scurrying by Zoe's feet. She scooped the animal up and nudged it into the pet carrier with Zak, ready to move. "But why? Who would single him out?"

"Sometimes it's about food," Paolo explained. "If they don't have enough hay to eat then it might cause the guinea pigs to turn on each other. But we know that isn't the case here – there's always plenty of hay around. So maybe there's a little bit of bullying going on as the boys try to establish who's in charge."

Zoe thought about Sinbad the lion, roaring to let everyone know he was the alpha male of his little pride, and wondered whether Tindu would act the same way when Koko arrived – the last thing Tanglewood needed was more tiger trouble. But it was perfectly possible that Tindu and Koko wouldn't be friends; animals of the same species didn't always get along when they lived together, as the guinea pigs seemed to be proving.

"So that's why you're moving some of them," she said. "But how do you know whether you're taking the bully too?"

"I've been watching them and I think the culprit is Micky over there," Paolo said, pointing to a brown and white guinea pig in the corner. "But it isn't fair to move Zak all by himself. You know how sociable these guys are."

Zoe nodded – she remembered how lonely little Fluff had been when he'd damaged his leg not long after she'd joined Team GP. He'd squeaked for joy when Max had finally reunited him with his furry friends.

"I'll keep an eye on things," she told Paolo. "Where are you moving them to?"

"One of the empty rabbit pens," Paolo said, pointing to a small grassy enclosure further along the path. "It does mean we'll have two sets of guinea pigs to clean out, though. Double the work."

Zoe stepped closer. "I don't mind," she said, running a gentle hand over Zak's bald patch. "Not if it means this little guy is safe."

When Paolo had chosen enough guinea pigs to move with Zak, Zoe shepherded the remaining animals into the far end of the pen and closed it off. Then she started to clean out their living area while Paolo prepared a new home for the others. Once Zoe had replaced the sawdust, topped up the hard food pellets and refilled the water, she sprinkled a mixture of vegetables around. Remembering the meerkat treats they'd made earlier, she hid some carrot slices in the middle of the hay and stuck some into hard to reach places. Then she let the guinea pigs back in, laughing as they squeaked and meeped with pleasure.

"Careful, Digger," she said, as a gold-and-black guinea pig ran over her foot in his determination to reach a cabbage leaf. "There's plenty for everyone!"

She walked along to the path to the empty rabbit enclosure. The guinea pigs seemed just as happy in their new home. Zoe stood outside and watched the furry little creatures for a while, making sure there were no signs of fighting.

"They're getting along great now," she said.

"Good," Paolo said, looking pleased. "Fingers crossed that's the end of the problems."

After reaching down to deliver an extra tickle to Zak, she waved goodbye to Paolo and headed over to Tindu's den.

She bumped into Cassie on the way.

"Hi, Zoe," the big-cat keeper said, smiling. "You're just the person I was looking for."

"Am I?" Zoe asked. "Why?"

Cassie held up a spray bottle filled with a brown liquid. "I thought you might like to help me with this."

"I'd love to," Zoe said. "Um…what is it?"

Cassie laughed. "It's water mixed with cinnamon. I'm going to spray it on the trees and rocks in Tindu's enclosure to see if it's enough to tempt him outside. And since scent-marking was your idea, I thought you could join me."

Zoe felt a thrill of excitement. "In the habitat Mom designed?"

"Yes, although Tindu will obviously be safely indoors while we do it."

"I'd love to help," Zoe said, beaming. Then she thought about Oliver – he wouldn't want to miss this. "But it wasn't just my idea – Oliver and I came up with scent-marking together. Have you asked him to help too?"

Cassie nodded. "He's on zebra duty and won't be free until later. Unfortunately, your dad wants us to try this as soon as possible, so it can't wait."

Poor Oliver, Zoe thought. *He must be disappointed to be missing out.* But Tindu's welfare had to come first. "Okay, what do you need me to do?"

Cassie reached into her baggy pockets and pulled out another spray bottle. "Take this and I'll show you."

The outdoor habitat felt bigger than Zoe was expecting. Her nerves tingled as she stepped into the space for the first time and double-checked the hatch was closed: it was. At the far end of the enclosure, there was a rocky outcrop which overlooked a shallow pool. Zoe guessed those would be the heated rocks her mother had included in the design. She could easily imagine Tindu stretched out on them, in full view of the toughened glass safety windows. There were plenty of other vantage points for the tiger. All big cats liked to be able to climb up high and keep an eye on what was happening down below. There was a climbing pole too, which reminded Zoe of a giant scratching post. And she saw plants and greenery everywhere, although she only really recognized the bamboo.

"If you start at that end, I'll go to the other one and we'll meet in the middle," Cassie suggested. "Spray it in places you think Tindu might be able to smell it but don't overdo things – we don't want to overwhelm him."

Zoe began with small patches here and there – underneath leaves and halfway up the trees. She had great fun climbing up to the high platforms to spray the cinnamon liquid on the wooden poles and tried to imagine how Tindu might react. Would he love the spicy smell as much as they hoped?

"All done," she called to Cassie.

"Good work," the keeper replied. "Now let's see if it works."

They made their way out of the enclosure. Zoe waited on the path while Cassie made sure the gates were all securely locked. Then the two of them walked back to the tiger house, where Tindu was pacing around behind the bars with his head hung low. Cassie used the pulley system to open the hatch leading to the outdoor enclosure and Zoe crossed her fingers that the smell would tempt the tiger.

For a moment or two, it seemed Tindu hadn't noticed the spicy scent. Then his pacing slowed and he stopped to stare at the hatch. Growling softly, he padded towards it. Zoe clenched her fists. *Go on*, she told the tiger silently. *Go on*.

"Look!" Cassie murmured. "When he bares his teeth and dangles his tongue like that, he's smelling through his mouth. It's called a flehmen response."

Zoe looked more closely – Tindu had his eyes half closed and he really did seem to be soaking up the richly spiced air. She watched, willing him on, and thought she would burst with excitement when he slunk through the hatch. Cassie flashed her a triumphant look.

"I'll leave the hatch open so that he understands he's not trapped outside," she whispered.

Zoe nodded. The minutes ticked by and Tindu didn't reappear. She wanted to watch him outside but she knew her sudden appearance might disturb him, so instead, she tried to imagine what he might be doing – rubbing against the cinnamon-scented trees, perhaps, or splashing around in the pool with the big, specially strengthened plastic ball Cassie had left there. They waited a few more hopeful minutes, until there was a flash of orange and black at the hatch and the tiger was back, his fur bone dry, meaning he hadn't even dipped a paw into the pool. He began pacing once more, showing no further interest in venturing outside.

Zoe sighed in disappointment but Cassie looked pleased. "It's a start," she said. "Now he knows it's safe out there, he might go and explore again."

"I suppose so," Zoe said.

"Thanks for all your help," Cassie said, smiling. "I'm sure Tindu appreciates it too."

Zoe was lost in thought as she made her way back to the manor. So many of the other animals were enjoying being outside; the ring-tailed lemurs were chasing each other along the looping ropes that hung from the enclosure roof, the otters were splashing in the water and the goats seemed to love leaping around the obstacles in their pen. What Cassie needed was something irresistible to help Tindu see his new home was the perfect place for him. But she didn't know what that something might be; food wasn't working and he didn't seem interested in toys – the tiger ball was right where Cassie had placed it. He didn't even want to try the pool. Zoe huffed in frustration; if only they could make him feel comfortable outside the den...

She rounded the corner of the manor and made her way towards the back door. A movement behind the trash cans caught her eye and she stopped. Peering out from behind one of the metal barrels was a scowling orange face: the tabby cat!

Zoe considered her next move. If she hurried towards the animal, she might scare it away.

"Hey, kitty," she called in a low voice. "Are you hungry again?"

She moved with deliberate care towards the back door, keeping her gaze fixed on the cat, and edged inside the kitchen.

Her mother was stirring a pan of chili on the stove.

"There you are," she said. "I was wondering where you were."

"Do we have any tuna?" Zoe asked, peering into the pantry.

Mom frowned. "There's an open can in the fridge. But your dinner will be ready in a moment."

"It's not for me," Zoe said, hurrying to the refrigerator. "There's a stray cat outside. I think it's hungry."

"A stray?" Mom said, looking surprised. "But where could it have come from?"

Zoe scooped the tuna onto a saucer, then filled another with water and headed for the door. "I don't know, but it's been hanging around for a few days. If I can get closer, I might be able to see if it's wearing a collar with a tag."

Zoe slipped out of the back door, leaving it open, and searched for a glimpse of orange behind the trash cans. The cat was still there, watching her. Zoe put both saucers down and quickly stepped back, keeping her distance so that the tabby wouldn't feel threatened.

After a moment or so, the cat began to edge

forwards. Casting its head from side to side nervously, it took a few halting steps and then ran towards the food and began to gulp it down. Tears pricked at Zoe's eyes as she watched; it was small – probably a girl, although it was hard to tell just by looking – and painfully thin. She could see its ribs beneath the dull fur and it had an angry red gash near one ear, as though it had been in a fight. There was no collar.

"I think you've had a difficult time," she murmured softly. "You poor thing."

The cat's ears flickered back at the sound of her voice but it didn't run away. Once the saucer with the tuna was licked clean, it turned to the water and lapped delicately until that saucer was empty too. Then it looked at the open back door and hesitated. Zoe didn't move, crossing her fingers that the animal would go inside. If it had been someone's pet then the temptation of a warm comfortable house might be too strong to resist.

But then Rory clattered into the kitchen, singing

loudly, and the spell broke. The cat looked up, baring its teeth in a terrified hiss. It spun around and raced across the grass before Zoe could even open her mouth. It vanished among the trees, leaving her to wonder what might have happened if Rory hadn't chosen that exact moment to appear. With a heavy sigh, she went into the house. What was it Cassie had said? *The quickest way to an animal's heart was through its stomach.* If that was true then it looked like Zoe was going to need a lot more tuna.

Chapter Five

Zoe got up early on Tuesday morning, but this time it wasn't so that she could observe Tindu on the cameras. She rummaged around in the pantry until she found a can of sardines and put some on a saucer outside the back door. After school, she was pleased to see the sardines were gone and she was confident that the stray had eaten them.

She loaded up another plate with fish and placed it beside the back door. This time she had barely put the food down when the cat came running. Zoe stepped back into the kitchen and waited until all the sardines were gone. Was it her imagination or was the tabby's fur a little less dull now? It was hard to tell but the cat was definitely curious about the open back door. Mom was at a meeting but Zoe had learned her lesson from the night before. She'd told Dad about the cat and asked him to keep Rory busy somewhere else in the house. The kitchen was completely empty – perfect for an inquisitive kitty to explore.

She expected the cat to panic when she appeared in the doorway but it simply stopped and stared at her for a moment, then continued lapping up the last few flakes. Remembering the way Cassie had left the den door open in the tiger house, to allow Tindu to control whether he was in or out, she left the back door as it was and took a seat at the kitchen table. The cat practically ignored her as it licked the plate.

A few minutes passed. Then the cat poked a wary

nose around the door. Zoe held her breath as it padded inside. Every now and then its ears pricked up or flattened at an unexpected noise or thud from elsewhere in the house, but it showed no signs of running away.

She sent a quick message to her dad: *The cat is in the kitchen. Now what?*

I left you a pet carrier, Dad replied. *See if you can get the cat inside so we can check to see if it's microchipped.*

A lot of pet owners had tiny microchips put harmlessly just under the animal's skin so that they could be reunited if they got lost. Zoe hoped that this cat would belong to one of them. She scraped out the last few sardines from the bottom of the can onto a piece of foil and placed it inside the pet carrier on the floor. The cat hovered uncertainly outside the plastic crate for a moment. Zoe held her breath. It placed one timid paw inside and sniffed the air. Then it dipped its head and followed its nose.

Quickly, Zoe closed the door and the cat hissed.

"Sorry, kitty," Zoe said, bending down to gaze into the carrier. "But we can't get you home without doing this."

Pulling out her phone, she sent a message to her dad: *Mission completed!*

A few minutes later, Dad appeared in the kitchen doorway, with Rory peering around his legs.

"Good work," Dad said, taking in the scene. "Did you have any trouble?"

"No," Zoe replied. "I think she's used to being in a pet carrier."

Dad came closer. "I think it's a girl too, even though orange tabby cats are usually male – the boys usually have larger heads and this cat is pretty small and delicate. But Max will find out for sure."

"I want to come," Rory said immediately.

"Not this time," Dad said in a firm tone. "Max will want to do some tests to see how healthy this cat is. There'll be a lot of waiting around. Why don't we find Mommy instead? I think she's over at the wolf enclosure."

They dropped Rory off with Mom and hurried over to the medical center. On the way, Dad's expression grew serious.

"I need to warn you that there are a number of illnesses a stray cat might pick up," he said as they walked. "The cut on this cat's head suggests he or she has been in a fight, which is how a lot of diseases are transmitted. Some of them can be serious, even life-threatening."

Zoe glanced down at the pet carrier in her hand. *Please be okay*, she thought, trying not to imagine what would happen if the tabby did have a serious disease.

"Even if it turns out to be healthy, it will need to spend a few days in isolation while we treat it," Mr. Fox went on. "It looks very dehydrated and will need some antibiotics in case that wound is infected."

"That might give us enough time to find its owner," Zoe said. "If there's no microchip."

Max and Oliver were waiting at the medical center.

"Is that the cat we saw last week?" Oliver asked.

Zoe nodded and placed the pet carrier onto the rubber-coated examination table. "I put some food down to get it to trust me."

"A little like we're trying to do with Tindu," Oliver said. "I hope it works for him too."

"So this is the mysterious stray Oliver told me about," Max said as he snapped on a pair of gloves and opened the door to let the cat out. "Let's take a look at you, then."

It took a moment for the cat to poke its head outside, and when it did, Zoe saw that its ears were flat against its head, suggesting it was unhappy.

"I think you've been to the vet's before," she said, watching its tail swish angrily. "You recognize the smell."

Carefully, she stroked the orangey head, tickling its furry ears until it relaxed a little and sniffed its way out. Zoe smiled; the tabby really was super-cute…

Max waited until the cat was completely clear of the carrier, then lifted the box away. Gently, he began to examine the cat. "It's a female," he said as his fingers moved over the animal's body. "Very thin. I'd say she's been lost about two or three weeks and she's had a few battles by the looks of things."

He held a stethoscope over the cat's heart and listened. "Strong pulse, though, which is a good sign." He smiled at Zoe. "It's a good thing you found her when you did."

Worry plucked at Zoe's heart as she gazed at the little cat. "Dad says she might have a disease."

Max's smile faded. "That's quite likely. We'll need to run some tests. But before that, we need to see if she's chipped."

He grabbed the reader and passed it over the cat's neck. Nothing happened. "No chip," he said with a disappointed sigh. "Which makes finding her owner a lot more difficult."

"I can make some posters," Zoe said instantly. "We can put them up around the park, in case anyone recognizes her."

"Yeah, I'll help," Oliver said. "We can do flyers too so people can spread the word."

Mr. Fox nodded. "While you get those started, we'll need to check her health. But the good news is that it won't take long." Max touched the cat's head and she closed her eyes as she rubbed against his hand. "We can give her an IV to help with her dehydration and malnutrition, plus treat her for ticks and fleas. Why don't you come back in the morning before school for an update?"

Zoe hesitated. Now that she'd found the cat, she was reluctant to leave her. But she knew it was for the best – the tabby needed to be kept away from other animals in case she was infectious, and some rest in a warm, safe place would do her a lot of good.

"Okay," she said, swallowing a sigh and reaching out to tickle the cat's ears. "Bye, kitty."

"She doesn't have a name," Oliver said suddenly. "What are we going to call her?"

Zoe saw her dad and Max exchange a worried look. She knew what they were thinking – there was no point in naming the cat if the test results were bad news. But Zoe had a soft spot for the little cat already and she deserved a name, even if she couldn't stay at Tanglewood.

She glanced at Oliver: the last time they'd been given the chance to name a Tanglewood animal, he'd chosen the name. But now he held up his hands. "You found her. It's up to you."

Zoe gazed at the tabby thoughtfully. "I think you should be called Lucky."

Max smiled. "It's the perfect name. Come on, Lucky, let's find you a nice warm bed for the night."

Zoe watched as he nudged the cat back into the animal carrier. She let out a heartbreaking meow as he took her away.

"Bye," Zoe called. "I'll come and see you tomorrow."

"First Tindu and now Lucky," Oliver said, shaking his head. "Tanglewood has been all about cats recently!"

He was right, Zoe thought, as she washed her hands. It did feel as though everyone's attention had been focused on cats lately. But of course everyone was worried about Tindu – Sumatran tigers were an endangered species; he was a Very Important Cat. Lucky was only a stray but that didn't mean she wasn't important too. Zoe thought the tabby was plucky and brave – she deserved just as much TLC as her big-cat cousin. And Zoe was determined to do whatever she could to help them both.

The next morning, Zoe slipped into the park early, long before most of the keepers had arrived. She'd found it hard to get to sleep the night before and when she had finally nodded off, she'd had a dream that Koko had turned up early all on her own and had chased Tindu all around Tanglewood. Zoe had been very glad to wake up.

"You're up early," Libby the animal nurse said when Zoe walked into the medical center. "I expect you're here to see the little stray you found."

Zoe nodded. "How is she?"

"Not bad," Libby said. "She had a good night,

although she doesn't like having an IV in her paw! She keeps trying to pull it out; we've had to put a cone on her neck to stop her from chewing at the bandages."

Surely that's a good sign? Zoe thought as she followed the nurse through to the isolation room. If Lucky wasn't feeling well she wouldn't have the strength to chew at the bandages holding the IV in place. Her Auntie Nina used to have a cat and Zoe remembered it had needed a cone after an operation too.

Once she got close to the spacious pen Lucky was being kept in, she could see that Max and his team had cleaned up the cut on her head. There was a small neat bald patch where they'd shaved the fur away and Zoe saw the wound was healing. There was an empty bowl in the corner of the box, and at the other end there was a small litter tray which looked as though it had been recently used. *Another good sign*, Zoe thought hopefully.

"As you can see, there's nothing wrong with her appetite," Libby said, grinning.

"I think it's been a while since she ate regularly," Zoe said. "Do you have the results of the tests Max ran?"

Libby nodded. "Yes. But you'll need to wait for Max to arrive to find out what they are. I'm sure he won't be long."

He'd probably be making sure Oliver ate his breakfast before school, Zoe thought. She checked the time – it wasn't even eight o'clock yet, still plenty of time before she had to catch the bus. She could afford to wait a few minutes for Max.

Lucky bashed the plastic cone against the side of the box and let out a sad-sounding meow. Zoe smiled in sympathy.

"It doesn't look very comfortable," she told the cat. She glanced over at Libby. "Is it okay if I play with her a little while I wait for Max?"

"Sure," Libby said, smiling. "She's actually really friendly. I think she'd love some company."

There wasn't much Zoe could do with Lucky, not while her paw was still connected to the IV and the plastic cone was around her neck, so she stuck to stroking the cat's bony back through a small opening in the top of the pen and tickling her under the chin. Lucky especially liked her ears being rubbed and soon began to purr, making Zoe even more certain she was somebody's pet.

"Don't worry," she told the cat as the purring grew louder. "We'll find your owner somehow."

Max arrived a few minutes later.

"Good morning, Zoe," he said briskly. "How's the patient today?"

"She seems much brighter," Zoe said. "Libby says she doesn't like the IV, though."

Max checked the plastic bag dangling from the IV stand beside the cage. "Well, the good news is that we can probably take that out."

Zoe bit her lip. Did that mean the test results showed Lucky didn't have any illnesses? Or was it a sign that Max felt she was showing signs of getting better? "Really?"

"Yes. She's nowhere near as dehydrated as she

was and she's eating well."

"What about her test results?" Zoe asked anxiously.

"Hey, don't look so glum," Max said, reaching across to pat her arm. "The results look good. Lucky needs to be kept indoors for a few weeks to be certain but she tested negative for feline leukemia and the immune system diseases. She's a little bit under the weather because of all the fleas she was carrying but we're treating her for that too."

Zoe felt a burst of relief; it sounded as though Lucky was going to be okay. "So we should start trying to find her owner?"

Max smiled. "That sounds like a very good idea to me."

"Don't worry," Zoe said, reaching in to pet Lucky's head again. "I'm going to do everything I can to get you back home."

And if no one comes forward to claim her, Zoe thought as she tickled the cat's chin, *maybe I'll be allowed to keep her myself.*

"Zoe, you'd better wash your hands and get going," Max said, tilting his head at the clock on the wall. "The school bus will be here soon!"

"Eek!" Zoe squeaked, closing the top of the isolation pen and hurrying over to the sink. She washed as fast as she could, then scooped her bag onto her shoulder. "See you later, Max! See you later, Lucky!"

Chapter Six

After school, Oliver offered to help Zoe make some "Have You Lost This Cat?" posters.

"We should take Lucky's photograph," Oliver said. "Someone might recognize those orange stripes."

Zoe nodded. "Good plan. I want to check on her anyway – let's go to the medical center now."

Lucky started purring almost the moment Zoe opened the top of her pen. The IV and the cone were both gone.

"Aw, did you miss me?" Zoe asked, running her hand all the way from Lucky's head to the tip of her orange tail. The fur felt soft and warm beneath her fingers, although the bones of the animal's spine were still obvious, making Zoe wish she'd found her sooner.

"I think she has missed you," Libby said. "She's been mewing all day."

Zoe's smile dipped in concern. "Oh, is she okay?"

"She likes company," Libby said. "I think she's lonely out here on her own, although we try to pop in to see her when we can."

Zoe sighed and petted the cat's soft fur again.

"I wish I could stay with her all the time," she said. "But we're going to make some posters tonight to try to find her owner. I'm sure she must have one – look how friendly she is."

"Speaking of posters, say cheese, Lucky," Oliver said, holding up his phone to snap a picture through the open flap at the top of the pen. "You're going to be famous."

It didn't matter how many times Zoe told herself it was important to get started on the posters, she found it hard to drag herself away from the purring cat – Lucky was just so friendly and cute. But Zoe knew she had to do what was right for the stray, and that meant trying to locate her owner. Someone, somewhere, might be missing Lucky just as much as the little tabby was missing them.

"Want to go over and see Tindu?" Oliver asked, as they got closer to the tiger house.

Zoe glanced at her watch. She and Oliver both had homework to do and all three parents had insisted it was done before they could make a start on the posters. "I suppose five minutes will be okay."

They had to pass Big Cat Mountain to get to Tindu's enclosure. Cassie was giving a talk on Sinbad and Suki and the other African lions at Tanglewood.

"African lions are a vulnerable species. Like all big cats, they're at risk from poachers," Cassie was saying. "But they're not critically endangered like the Sumatran tiger. They desperately need our help to survive, which is why we're holding a Terrific Tigers fundraising weekend next week. With a little bit of luck you'll even be able to meet our new Tanglewood tigers, Tindu and Koko."

Interested mumbling broke out among the visitors. Zoe glanced across at Tindu's enclosure, still hidden from public view by fences, and felt a quiver of anxiety. So much depended on Tindu settling in; Koko couldn't come if he didn't. How could they have a tiger weekend with no tigers?

Cassie finished her talk and answered several questions about Sinbad and Suki and the rest of the pride. The crowd began to drift away and Cassie came over to Oliver and Zoe.

"If you two are hoping to see Tindu, I'm afraid you're out of luck," she said. "Max is in with him now, observing his pacing behavior, and he said strictly no interruptions."

Oliver looked disappointed and Zoe understood why – they were both hoping Tindu might be showing signs of perking up. But if the tiger was still pacing his den, it didn't sound as though he was any happier.

"Come on," Oliver said, sighing. "Let's go and make a start on these posters."

Oliver stayed for dinner and after finishing their homework, spent most of that evening working with Zoe, designing posters to print off. They planned to put them up all over the park the moment they got home from school on Thursday. Mrs. Fox helped to upload Lucky's details to several lost-pet websites, too.

"I'm sure we'll find Lucky's owner soon," she said. "You're doing a great job."

"Let's print off some flyers, like you suggested," Zoe said to Oliver. "We can hand them out in the cafe."

"Rory is going to a birthday party in the soft-play area on Friday afternoon, for a little girl from his preschool," Mom said. "There'll be lots of local families around then too."

Zoe reached for the laptop. "So what are we waiting for?"

The park was busy on Friday afternoon. Zoe had been delighted by the number of visitors who'd offered to help spread the word since she and Oliver had started putting the posters up. There were some posters in the cafe too, which was packed with parents and children. One corner had been fenced off and the tables were piled with cups and plates, with silver and blue balloons dotted in between. "Happy Birthday, Mia!" banners had been draped across the windows, and a multicolored piñata shaped like a number four hung from the ceiling. Zoe grinned – the party-goers were going to have fun with that!

Most of the children were running around the soft-play area. Rory kicked off his shoes the moment he arrived and went inside to join them.

"Wow," Oliver said, gazing around at the busy cafe. "I've never see it so full."

Zoe glanced at her mother. "Is it okay for us to give out the flyers?"

Mom smiled. "Of course. I'll mention it to some of the parents too."

Zoe and Oliver worked their way around, handing out flyers and explaining Lucky's story. Most were sympathetic but no one recognized the cat. Once everyone had a flyer, Oliver turned to Zoe. "I think I'll take a walk around the park and give some more of these out."

"Okay," Zoe said. "I'll come and find you in a little while. I want to see them do the piñata first."

The noise levels grew louder and louder. Finally, Mia's mom called all the party-goers over. "Piñata time! Come and line up over here."

There was a stampede of feet as the children hurried over. Music started to play and they danced around as they waited for their turn to hit the straw number four, cheering as it swung wildly. Rory landed a hefty thump but the piñata didn't break. It wasn't until each child had tried at least one hit that the straw began to give way and the glistening candy wrappers started to show. Finally, the birthday girl found a weak spot and the candy rained down. Zoe couldn't help laughing as the children scrambled around, scooping up the shiny wrappers. They reminded her of meerkats scrabbling around after insects, desperate to grab as many as they could!

It was time for the party games next. Zoe waited until Rory was settled at the circle and passing a brightly wrapped package before saying bye to her mom and going to find Oliver.

The late-afternoon crowds seemed wowed by Tanglewood – Zoe was delighted to hear so much praise and excitement as she handed out her flyers. As usual, Flash was proving to be a big attraction; Jenna was doing a zebra talk outside their enclosure and Zoe saw a number of children in the audience whose faces were painted with black and white stripes.

"They have so many awesome animals here," Zoe heard one boy say to his mother. "It's so much better than the last time we came!"

"The Terrific Tigers weekend sounds great,"

the woman said, pointing to a nearby poster with pictures of Tindu and Koko. "They're my favorite animals."

The boy gave her a pleading look. "Can we come back? Please, Mom, can we?"

The woman laughed. "Okay, we can come."

Zoe smiled, in spite of her anxiety over whether the tigers would be ready in time for the weekend. This was the third time she'd overheard people talking about Tindu and Koko and it was great to see visitors so excited about the park's newest animals. She took a few steps closer and handed the woman a flyer. "Excuse me but I don't suppose you recognize this cat, do you? We found her on the grounds and we're trying to find her owner."

The woman and her son squinted at the flyer, then shook their heads. "Sorry."

"No worries, enjoy the rest of your visit," Zoe said, swallowing a sigh. No one seemed to know Lucky.

Oliver was over by Big Cat Mountain, where more visitors were admiring Sinbad and Suki sunning themselves on the highest rock. The other three female lions, Selina, Ninky and Ariele, were prowling around the entrance to their den, and Zoe guessed it must be almost feeding time. The big cats at Tanglewood were fed once every three days, to replicate the way they might hunt and eat in the wild. From the looks of things, today was the turn of the lions.

"Have you had any luck with the flyers?" Zoe asked Oliver.

He shook his head. "One lady thought it might be her cat who went missing a month ago but that was a male."

"Oh," Zoe said, disappointed. "Well, I suppose it might take some time to find Lucky's owner."

"Yeah. I've run out of flyers now," Oliver said.

"Me too."

Oliver glanced towards the tiger territory, hidden behind its temporary wooden fencing. "Dad says we're allowed to visit Tindu today. Want to go and see if there's anything we can do to help Cassie?"

Zoe hesitated – part of her wanted to go back to the house to print off more flyers. But the crowds would be back again in the morning; maybe it was better to wait for fresh faces. "Okay. I've heard lots of people talking about the fundraising weekend – fingers crossed Tindu is feeling more at home."

Oliver nodded. "Yeah, I heard a few people too. I hope the scent-marking has helped."

The door to the tiger house was shut. Oliver tapped lightly on the glass and a moment later, Cassie appeared to let them in.

"Hello, you two," she said cheerfully. "Have you come to check up on Tindu?"

Zoe nodded, then paused. She could hear the sound of voices – someone somewhere seemed to be having a conversation about visiting the pyramids in Egypt. "Do you have the radio on?" she asked in confusion.

Cassie smiled. "Yes. I thought it might help get Tindu used to the noise of the crowds. I realized he was used to having plenty of visitors at his old home and wondered if things were a little too quiet in here – when the doors are closed you can't hear much of what's going on outside. So I found an old radio to leave on for background noise, in case he misses the sound of people talking."

Tindu was prowling around his section of the den. Every now and then his gaze flickered towards Zoe, Oliver and Cassie, but he didn't stop pacing back and forth.

"How is he?" Oliver asked.

"Still unsettled," Cassie admitted with a sigh. "I thought we'd made a breakthrough after Zoe and I sprayed cinnamon around his enclosure – he came out of the den and explored a little. But he's shown no interest since, not even when we hid food around it."

"He liked the cinnamon smell," Zoe said slowly. "Maybe you could try more of that? Lay a trail that led to something irresistible."

Cassie looked thoughtful. "His last keepers said he likes salmon so we tried to tempt him with that.

But he doesn't respond when we leave any kind of food out for him."

Zoe thought hard. In the wild, a tiger might have to stalk and hunt their prey. They needed ingenuity and cunning if they wanted to eat. Perhaps Tindu didn't want his food to come too easily. What they needed to do was come up with a way to entice him out of the den and provide a challenge all at the same time…

A memory flashed into her head of the meerkat treats they'd made the week before; the meerkats had needed to dig and scrabble for their snacks. Obviously that wouldn't work for Tindu because his food wasn't alive, but what if there was a way to make it feel as though his food was moving? And suddenly, she had an idea.

"What if we gave him a piñata?" she said in excitement. "We could fill it with his favorite food?"

Cassie stared at Zoe. "And we could lay a cinnamon trail too, to encourage him to find it."

Zoe imagined Tindu prowling through the

enclosure, tracking his food, and grinned. "Yes! What do you think? Could it work?"

"You know what, it might," Cassie said. "Great idea, Zoe. I'll make the piñata tonight."

"We could make it," Oliver offered, then he hesitated. "At least, I think we could. I've never made one before."

"I have," Zoe said. "We made papier-maché shapes at my old school using some old newspaper and glue."

"That's right," Cassie said, smiling. "Except glue isn't safe so you'll need to make a flour and water paste to stick everything together. Or you could decorate a cardboard box."

Zoe nodded hard. "We could definitely do it. When would you like us to bring it over to you?"

Cassie glanced over at Tindu, who was still pacing back and forwards. "As soon as you can. Papier maché needs plenty of time to dry, but if you made it tonight, you could bring it over tomorrow. Then you'll be able to stay to see if it works."

Zoe and Oliver exchanged a determined look.

"It's a deal," Oliver said. "Don't worry, Tindu, you're going to love it!"

Chapter Seven

Zoe made a detour to the medical center on her way home, to say goodnight to Lucky. The cat was happy to see her, as always, her whole body vibrating with a purr that seemed too loud for such a small animal.

"We handed out lots of flyers today," Zoe told her. "We might have some news about your owner soon."

She jiggled the toy mouse that was lying on the

floor of the pen, smiling as Lucky leaped at it. The little cat was *so* adorable.

Libby came into the isolation room. "You're going to miss her when you find her owner."

"Mmm," Zoe said, wiggling the toy again. "I almost hope we don—"

She stopped suddenly and felt her cheeks grow hot. Had she really been about to say that she hoped they *didn't* find Lucky's owner? That wasn't fair for anyone – if Lucky was Zoe's cat, she'd be sick with worry if she went missing, and Lucky deserved to go back to the home she knew. Libby gave her a keen-eyed look and Zoe busied herself with replacing the cat's water, waiting for her face to stop burning.

"Do you think Mom and Dad would let me keep her?" she asked Libby a few minutes later. "If no one comes forward to claim her, I mean."

"You'd have to ask them," Libby replied. "But she will need to find a new home once she's better. We can't keep her here."

"But there's no reason I couldn't keep her," Zoe persisted. "If Mom and Dad say I can?"

Libby smiled. "I think you'd make the perfect owner for Lucky. But as I said, it isn't up to me."

Zoe replaced Lucky's food and finished cleaning up her pen, deep in thought. Of course the best thing for Lucky would be to go back to the home she'd known before, but what if they couldn't find her owner? Maybe her parents would let Lucky stay, instead of looking for a new home with strangers? She tickled the cat's ears, loving the way her eyes closed in appreciation. Surely it made sense to keep Lucky here, where she was already loved?

Giving the cat one last pet before closing the pen, Zoe made up her mind to ask her parents if she could keep Lucky. Then she'd be able to give the tabby the home she deserved.

Mrs. Fox was in the bathroom upstairs, giving Rory a bath before bed.

"Give it some time," she said, when Zoe asked about Lucky. "You only put the posters up yesterday."

"But if no one claims her – can we keep her then?"

Mom sighed as Rory splashed around in the bubbles. "I knew this would happen. Don't we have enough animals to look after at Tanglewood, without adding another one?"

Zoe took a deep breath. "You know how much I love helping out. But it's not the same as having a pet of my own. I can't cuddle with Tindu!"

"True," Mrs. Fox said. She stared hard at Zoe for a moment. "Okay, let me talk to Dad about it."

"Yes!" Zoe cried, punching the air in delight.

Mom shook her head. "Don't get too excited. If Dad says no then that's the end of it, understood?"

"Of course," Zoe said, nodding. Her dad was sure to think it was a great idea.

"Grrrrr," Rory said, baring his teeth and splashing his hands in the water. "I'm Tindu. Grrr grrr grrr!"

Zoe remembered about the piñata. "Oh – do we have any thick cardboard? And maybe some newspaper?"

Her mother looked surprised. "I expect so. We've got plenty of old paper and empty boxes around."

"And some flour?"

"Probably," Mom said, frowning. "Why, what are you up to?"

Zoe tapped the side of her nose. "It's a surprise. You don't mind if Oliver comes over again tonight, do you?"

Mrs. Fox shrugged. "Of course not, he's always welcome. Do I even want to know what this is all about?"

"I'll tell you tomorrow," Zoe said. "Now, where did you say those boxes were?"

It turned out to be more difficult than Zoe had expected to make a piñata. While she and Oliver agreed that their piñata needed to dangle down to capture Tindu's interest, they couldn't decide on a shape or even a color.

"Tigers don't eat flamingos," Oliver pointed out, when Zoe held up the pink tissue paper she'd found in Rory's craft box.

They would, Zoe thought, *if they could catch one*.

"They don't eat elephants either," she said, dropping the paper back onto the kitchen table and sending a cloud of multicolored tissue pieces floating into the air. "But that didn't stop you from suggesting gray."

Oliver thought for a moment. "Does it really matter? Who says it has to be shaped like an animal, anyway? The most important thing is the scent."

"Good point," Zoe said. "Tindu won't care what it looks like. So why don't we tilt one of the boxes to make a diamond shape – something that's strong enough to withstand a few whacks from those heavy paws – and cover it in rainbow colors?"

Oliver picked up a ruler and a pencil and nodded. "Okay. Give it a try."

A little while later, they had a multicolored, diamond-shaped piñata that dangled and spun from the sturdy rope they had threaded through the top. It wasn't as well made as the one from Mia's party, but Zoe was sure it would do the trick.

"I think it looks pretty good," she said, squinting as Oliver held it up.

Oliver nodded. "Now all we need is a breeze to make it sway and catch Tindu's eye."

Zoe took a deep breath and blew the piñata, watching the tissue paper flutter as it twirled. "I don't think he's going to miss our piñata – and he's going to love the fishy treats inside."

"I hope so," Oliver said. "Let's keep our fingers crossed this will cheer him up. The Terrific Tigers weekend is almost here."

Zoe felt her stomach clench with worry. No one wanted to admit it but time was running out for Tindu; she knew her parents and Max and Cassie were worried that he wasn't eating. There was a danger that the tiger might never settle at Tanglewood

– that a new home might need to be found – and that would put Koko's arrival at risk too.

Zoe gnawed at her lip. The way things were going, Terrific Tigers was turning into Troublesome Tigers. The piñata idea just had to work. It *had* to!

Chapter Eight

Saturday morning dawned bright and clear, with just the hint of a breeze.

Zoe stopped by to see Lucky before heading over to meet Cassie and Oliver in the park. Dad had gone out early, and Mom said she hadn't had a chance to talk to him about adopting the little tabby. As much as Zoe tried not to get her hopes up, she couldn't help feeling a flicker of excitement when she saw how well Lucky was doing. Libby thought she might even be allowed out of the isolation room in the next few days, although she couldn't roam free. *And then*, Zoe thought, *you might be coming home with me.*

"You're such a smart kitty," she told Lucky, shaking the toy mouse and laughing as the cat pounced on it. "I wish I could spend the whole morning with you but there's a certain big cat who needs me, too."

Oliver was waiting outside the building where the keepers prepared the animal feeds with the piñata in his arms.

"I hope this works," he said.

"What do you think?" Zoe asked Cassie anxiously when she poked her head out of the building and summoned them inside. "Will Tindu like it?"

"Wow, that's bright!" the keeper said with a smile. She held up a bag of fish chunks. "And he's going to love the way it smells."

She led them into a small room packed with refrigerators, freezers and sinks. The smell of fish was strong as they carefully packed the piñata and sealed it shut. Then Cassie showed them how to mix the brown cinnamon powder with warm water over the sinks, pouring it into a plastic bottle and screwing a spray trigger on top. It was messy and the air was rich with the scent by the time they'd finished, with barely a hint of the fishy aroma they'd smelled earlier. Zoe's fingers were stained a dark chestnut brown. She resisted the temptation to lick them as she wrinkled her nose. "Cinnamon reminds me of apple pie."

"It reminds me of my mom," Oliver said quietly, rinsing his hands underneath the faucet.

Zoe shook the water from her own hands and tried to think of something to say. Oliver's mother had died a few years earlier and she knew he still missed her, although he didn't mention her often. She gave his arm a sympathetic squeeze.

"She'd be proud of you today," Cassie said with a warm smile. "I know she always hoped we'd have tigers at Tanglewood and using a piñata to tempt Tindu is such a great idea."

Oliver grunted. "It was Zoe's suggestion, not mine."

"But you're working together to make it happen," Cassie said. "Teamwork is important when you're looking after animals, especially big, dangerous cats like Tindu. You need to be able to trust the people you work with, and the two of you really do make a good team."

Zoe felt her cheeks grow hot with pride and glanced sideways at Oliver, wondering how he would feel about the keeper's comments.

"I suppose we do," he said, and flashed her a smile.

Once they had everything they needed, the three of them headed over to the tiger house. After double-checking that Tindu was safely inside his den and that the hatch leading outside was locked, Cassie let the three of them into the outdoor enclosure. This time, instead of spraying cinnamon on the trees and platforms, she laid a direct trail leading to one of the taller trees. Oliver climbed onto a nearby rock and

Zoe held the piñata up so that he could tie it to one of the branches.

"Make sure it's secure, about your dad's head height, Zoe," Cassie called. "We want it to challenge Tindu, remember – this way, he'll have to work for it."

When they were sure everything was ready, they left the enclosure and went into the tiger house. Cassie pulled the lever to open the hatch between Tindu's den and the outdoor habitat. Zoe followed the keeper as she slipped between the wooden fence keeping Tindu hidden from the public and the bars of the outer fence. They moved around until they had a clear view of the hatch and the piñata. Zoe nibbled at her nails, hoping they'd done enough to tempt the tiger out. Would the cinnamon do the trick? Would he be curious enough to try the piñata?

Zoe tried hard to keep absolutely still – she didn't want to spook Tindu. Beside her, Oliver was frozen to the spot too. And then, after a few tense minutes, the breath caught in Zoe's throat. Was that a flash of orange by the hatch? Yes, it was!

"Look!" Oliver whispered, as Tindu poked his muzzle outside and sniffed the air.

A moment later, the big cat was out. He swung his head from side to side, teeth bared, as though picking up the cinnamon trail Cassie had left for him. Seconds ticked by.

"Go on," Zoe breathed. "Follow the trail."

The tiger stopped and sniffed the air again, baring his teeth to allow the scent to reach his nostrils. Then he gazed around and seemed to spot the piñata as it gently swayed in the breeze. He froze.

"He's seen it," Zoe squeaked, barely able to contain her excitement. "Go on, Tindu."

"Ssshh," Oliver hissed, his eyes fixed on the tiger.

Slowly, Tindu turned towards the piñata. His belly sank towards the ground and he crept forwards a few more paces, eyes trained on the dangling box. He paused and Zoe dug her nails into her palm.

Go on, Tindu, she urged him silently.

Then the muscles in his powerful shoulders bunched and in a flash, he had covered the distance to the piñata and leaped up at it. The branch dipped and shook, then the piñata slipped out of his grip and bounced back up again.

Tindu stepped back warily and considered his prey once more. Instead of leaping up again, he reared up and reached out a paw, patting at the brightly colored diamond so that it swung back and forth. He swatted it again and the movement increased. Zoe felt an unexpected desire to giggle and clamped one hand over her mouth. The tiger reminded her of Lucky, playing with her toy mouse!

Tindu circled around and gazed upwards, planning his next move. A deep grumbling growl filled the air. Then suddenly, the tiger burst up onto his hind legs and used both paws to pull at the piñata. His claws flashed as they sank into the box. The branch bent and the cardboard gave way. The piñata fell to the ground. Tindu snarled and pounced on it, sinking his teeth into it and shaking it from side to side until it ripped open. The salmon pieces scattered.

Zoe squeezed her hands into fists. This was the

most important moment – would Tindu eat? She could hardly watch.

"Yes!" Cassie muttered beside her. "Go on, boy. Eat it all up now."

The tiger glanced around, his eyes wary. In the wild, he'd be watching out for other predators who might steal his kill, Zoe realized. Or maybe the other tigers at his old zoo had eaten more than their share, but there was no danger of anyone muscling in at Tanglewood. *Not until Koko arrives, anyway,* Zoe thought.

Tindu finished tearing at the cardboard, flipping the colorful pieces high into the air and shaking them until they fell apart. And then he bent his head to sniff at the fish.

Zoe heard Oliver suck in a deep breath. They all watched, waiting for Tindu to eat. He poked out his long tongue to lick at the salmon, then seemed to realize it was his favorite and began to gulp the fish chunks down. Cassie grinned in delight and held up a hand to high-five Zoe and Oliver.

Once he'd finished, Zoe expected Tindu to turn around and head back into the den, but instead, he leaped up onto one of the platforms and began to sniff.

"That's where I sprayed some cinnamon last week," Zoe whispered.

Cassie nodded, looking even more pleased. "He really seems to like that smell. Maybe we can use it to encourage him to eat from now on. Well done, guys. This is a real breakthrough."

Zoe and Oliver smiled at each other.

"You were right," Oliver said, shaking his head. "It didn't need to look like an elephant."

"Or a flamingo," Zoe said, laughing. "It turns out that tigers really like diamonds—"

"As long as they taste like salmon," Cassie finished.

Zoe's Dad and Max were amazed by the change in Tindu.

"I can't believe he's the same tiger," Mr. Fox said,

gazing through the bars in astonishment as Tindu batted his tiger ball along the ground as if he was nothing more than an overgrown kitten. "Excellent work, Cassie."

Cassie held up her hands. "Don't give me the credit – it's all due to Zoe and Oliver. They made the piñata."

Max managed to tear his eyes away from the magnificent sight of Tindu leaping from platform to platform and smiled. "That was an inspired idea. His old keepers said that Tindu has a mischievous nature – I think you've tapped into that."

"You should have seen him rip the piñata apart," Oliver said in an enthusiastic voice. "It was awesome."

"He's just like Lucky," Zoe said. "She loves playing with toys too."

Max laughed. "Yes, and I expect she'd enjoy a little salmon too. Little cats aren't so very different from big cats."

"And now that Tindu seems happier, we can

finalize our plans to move Koko into Tanglewood," Zoe's dad said. "Wait until you meet her – she's magnificent. In fact, I think she's going to run circles around Tindu."

"I wonder how he'll react," Oliver said. "Do you think he's going to like having another tiger around?"

Cassie looked thoughtful. "I hope so. He lived with other tigers at his old zoo so he might like having a friend. But there's a very real chance he might feel threatened – that's why we decided to introduce Koko as quickly as we could. Similarly, Koko might feel as though she has to establish her dominance over a new territory. She might pick a fight with Tindu on purpose."

"A lot depends on how well she travels and whether she settles in quickly," Mr. Fox said. "We'll have to take things one step at a time. And speaking of settling in, how is Lucky doing?"

Zoe felt her stomach clench. Had Mom spoken to Dad about Lucky, or was he just curious?

"She's doing well," Max said. "The wound on her

head is healing nicely and she's gaining weight. Any news about her owner yet?"

Zoe cleared her throat. "No. We've had a few emails from people who thought she might be theirs but nothing definite yet."

"It's still early days," Dad said. "Don't give up hope."

What would he say if he knew what I'm secretly hoping for? Zoe wondered uncomfortably.

"I think she'll be allowed out of isolation soon," Max said. "We'll have to find a temporary home for her then."

Zoe took a deep breath. "What happens if we never find her owner? Would she be able to stay at Tanglewood?"

Max looked troubled. "She's not out of the woods in terms of diseases yet – there's still a chance she could have something incubating. So Lucky can't be around other cats or go outside for another three months or so."

"But she could stay with us, couldn't she, Dad?"

Zoe said, aiming a pleading glance at her father. "If we were careful not to let her out of the house?"

Mr. Fox began to shake his head and Zoe knew Mom hadn't spoken to him. "Zoe—"

"It's not as though we have any other cats," she cut in. "So there's no risk there."

"No little cats," her dad said gently. "But there are some rather large cats here and they're just as at risk as their domestic cousins."

Zoe stared at him. He meant Tindu and Sinbad and Minty – all of Tanglewood's big cats. Was Lucky putting them all in danger?

"The chances of infection are very small," Max said. "It's also possible that Lucky is perfectly healthy. But you know how important Tindu is – numbers of Sumatran tigers are at critical levels worldwide and we can't risk him, or any of our big cats, catching anything."

"Think about it, Zoe," Dad said. "It's not unheard of for smaller animals to find their way into the bigger enclosures, especially at night, when our animals are safely in their pens. Lucky could easily creep into one of the big cat habitats and there's a very real chance she might pass on an infection through her saliva or urine. All she would need to do is lick a piece of meat or fish that another cat ate, or use an enclosure as a litter tray and they'd be in danger. I'm sorry, it's too risky."

Tears began to blur Zoe's vision. "So what are you saying? That she can't live anywhere?"

"No, of course not," her father said. "If her owner doesn't come forward then we'll find a home for her somewhere else, away from the park. Try to understand, Zoe – I have to do what's best for all the animals here at Tanglewood."

Zoe hung her head so that she didn't have to look at Tindu prowling around the enclosure. She'd formed a bond with Lucky and it didn't seem fair that they couldn't stay together. But Lucky was just a little stray cat – she didn't have the survival of her species resting on her shoulders the way Tindu did.

"I suppose so," she said eventually.

Dad smiled. "Good girl. And there's still a chance her owner will come to claim her. Then we won't need to worry about finding her a new home."

Zoe nodded and swallowed hard. If Lucky couldn't stay with her then the next best solution would be to reunite the cat with her own family, whoever that was. The problem was that there was no cinnamon trail to lead Zoe to Lucky's owners and she had no idea what to try next. No idea at all.

Chapter Nine

"It looks like the new living arrangements are working well."

It was Monday evening and Paolo was gazing over Zoe's shoulder at Zak the guinea pig, whose fur seemed to be growing back well.

"I think so," Zoe said, lowering the guinea pig to the ground so he could join his friends. She glanced over at the second enclosure. "None of the others seem to have lost any fur and both Micky and Zak look happy."

Paolo rubbed his chin, looking thoughtful. "I did wonder whether Micky had Zak so worried that he'd pulled his own fur out. It's not unheard of for stressed-out guinea pigs to do that."

Zoe watched the little animal nibble on a carrot and smiled. "He doesn't look stressed out now. I think he's happy in his new home."

"You're right," Paolo agreed. "I think we'll keep two guinea-pig pens from now on. And speaking of happy, I hear you played a big part in helping Tindu to settle into his new home."

Zoe felt her cheeks warm up. Paolo wasn't the first keeper to praise her for the way Tindu's confidence had apparently turned around. The tiger had started exploring the outdoor enclosure more and more, scent-marking different areas to warn other animals that this was his territory – in fact, he seemed to be enjoying his new home so much that his unsettled early days seemed like a bad dream. Zoe wasn't sure she could take much credit for the change in Tindu's mood but everyone seemed determined to compliment her for it.

"It was a team effort," she said, embarrassed. "We all chipped in with ideas."

Paolo smiled. "Well, whatever you did, it worked. And Cassie announced at today's staff meeting that Koko is arriving on Wednesday."

Zoe beamed. "I know – Dad told me. He says Cassie is happy that Tindu is settling in and doesn't want him to get too used to being on his own, in case it makes him resent Koko's arrival more."

"With some luck, it means that Tindu and Koko will be ready to wow the public this weekend," Paolo said. "Great job."

"I'm just glad Tindu is feeling settled enough for Koko to join him," Zoe said. "I was worried she wouldn't be able to come at all."

Paolo grimaced. "I think we all were. But it's all systems go."

Mentally, Zoe went over the dates. They weren't out of the woods yet: if Koko arrived on Wednesday, that gave Tanglewood's keepers less than two days to settle her in and to introduce her to Tindu before Terrific Tigers. What if Koko took as long as Tindu to feel at home? The outdoor enclosure was designed to be split into separate spaces, and there were three indoor dens in total, so if the worst came to the worst, the two tigers could be kept apart. But Tanglewood's visitors would be expecting to see them together.

Then another thought occurred to Zoe: what if Tindu and Koko didn't get along at *all*? The tigers had been carefully matched according to endangered species breeding programs and everyone was hoping for tiger cubs at some point in the future. Especially the public…

"I hope they make friends," Zoe said, blowing out a deep breath.

Paolo made a face. "Me too. It's one thing to maintain two living spaces for the guinea pigs but if the tigers don't get along then we're going to have a huge problem."

Zoe spent an hour playing with Lucky after school on Tuesday. The little stray was almost back to full strength and Max was happy enough with her recovery to let her out of isolation. Zoe sat on the floor in the medical center, rolling a little ball with a bell across the room and watching Lucky chase it and bat it along the floor. She even dug her claws into the plastic and rolled over, waving the ball in the air. Although Zoe laughed, she couldn't shake her worries about what might happen to the cat – now that she was better, Max and her dad would be thinking about rehoming her and Zoe didn't want to think about that. She knew they would make sure Lucky was going to a good home, but still…

She checked there was food and water in Lucky's new, much bigger pen, then patted her goodbye and headed over to the tiger enclosure. Everyone was excited about Koko's arrival the next day, but Zoe felt as though she hadn't gotten to know Tindu yet and wanted to spend a little more time watching him before his new housemate arrived. She ran into

Cassie outside the lemur enclosure. The big-cat keeper was wearing a baggy gray beanie hat and carrying a long stick with a round red blob on the end.

Zoe stared at it in bewilderment. "What are you planning to do with that?"

Cassie touched the silver whistle around her neck and smiled.

"Tiger training," she explained. "Now that Tindu is more comfortable with us I'm going to see how well he responds to some simple commands."

"What kind of commands?" Zoe asked, trying to imagine the big cat fetching a stick or rolling over when Cassie told him to.

"Nothing too complicated," Cassie replied. "You'll see what I mean if you join us, but basically it's so we can check up on him without having to sedate him. So one of the commands is designed to allow me to check whether his teeth are all healthy. Another is so that we can take blood from his tail if we need to do some tests."

"Wow," Zoe said, staring at the big-cat keeper. "I'd never really thought about how you'd do all of that."

Cassie waved her whistle. "I have this to help, and the beanie hat is a visual clue – his old keepers used to wear something similar so Tindu should know what's coming when he sees me." She patted the containers attached to her belt. "And of course I have my secret weapon."

"Let me guess," Zoe said. "Salmon, right?"

"Right," Cassie grinned. "So what do you think? Want to watch me put Tindu through his paces?"

Zoe nodded. "Definitely!"

Zoe could see the change in Tindu the moment she walked into the tiger house. He was still pacing his den but his head was no longer bowed and his eyes were bright and alert. His coat seemed sleeker and glossier too – even his whiskers seemed straighter! It was almost as though someone had traded him for a much happier tiger.

"Wow, he's so different," Zoe said, open-mouthed.

She pointed at the battered tiger ball on the floor inside the den. "It looks like he's got a favorite toy too, just like Lucky."

Cassie made a face. "Yes, now that he's more at home he loves his boomer ball. You should hear the racket he makes when he bangs it against the bars!"

The big-cat keeper unlocked the gate in the outer bars and stood beside the wire fence, while Zoe waited behind the first set of bars. Almost instantly, Tindu stopped pacing and stared at Cassie, his gaze watchful.

"We're using the same technique as his old keepers," Cassie explained, tugging a sliver of fish from the container attached to her belt. "I'm hoping he'll respond well."

Zoe stared in fascination as Tindu waited for instructions – he seemed to know what was coming even if Zoe didn't. Cassie gave one short, sharp blast on her whistle and then held the red ball high against the wire inner fence. "Come on, Tindu. Come on up."

Sure enough, a few seconds later Tindu reared up

and planted his massive paws against the metal wire. Cassie removed the ball and fed the salmon through a gap. Tindu gobbled it down. Next, Cassie placed the red ball much lower down, almost level with the concrete floor. Tindu flattened himself against the floor and Zoe noticed Cassie's hand gently pinching the top of the tiger's leg. She held it for a few seconds, then let go and removed the ball. Tindu ate the snack she offered and waited for his next instruction. This time, Cassie blew the whistle and tapped the ball at the tiger's head height.

"Open up," she told the tiger. "Let me see those teeth."

Tindu did as he was told, holding his mouth open for several long seconds. Zoe couldn't believe what she was seeing – it reminded her of a wildlife documentary she'd seen once, about tiny birds who flew into the mouths of crocodiles to clean their teeth – although she didn't suppose Tindu would keep his mouth open long enough for any work to be done.

"All we're doing here is training him," Cassie said,

as though reading Zoe's mind. "If he did have tooth trouble he'd need to be sedated before we could fix it. But forcing an animal to sleep is something we only do when we absolutely have to."

Cassie ran through each activity several times and Tindu responded each time. By the end of the training session, Zoe was in awe both of Cassie's training skills and Tindu's obedience.

"Thanks, Tindu," Cassie said, gazing deep into the tiger's intelligent amber eyes.

And then she did something Zoe hadn't seen her do before – she leaned forwards and made a strange half-blowing, half-hissing sound at Tindu. Even more amazingly, Tindu made the same sound back to her!

"What just happened?" Zoe managed after a few stunned seconds had passed. "Did you just... communicate with him?"

Cassie laughed. "In a way. It's called a chuffle. Tigers do it when they're happy, or to let other tigers know they're friendly."

Zoe frowned. "But you're not a tiger."

"Ah, but in a way I am," Cassie said, grinning. "Tindu and I understand each other. I suppose you could say we were thanking each other."

"Wow," Zoe breathed, gazing at Tindu in astonishment and making up her mind to try it with Lucky. "There's so much I don't know."

"Wait until Koko gets here," Cassie said. "It'll either be chuffle central or all-out war."

Zoe felt herself shiver with anticipation. Suddenly she couldn't wait for Koko to arrive. "I hope it's the first one. I don't think I could bear any more tension."

"Me neither," Cassie said. "Let's keep everything crossed that the two of them become best friends."

It was a wish that Zoe knew everyone at Tanglewood shared. Tomorrow, they'd know whether it was likely to come true.

Chapter Ten

Neither Zoe nor Oliver wanted to go to school on Wednesday. Zoe spent most of the day secretly checking her phone for news of Koko's arrival, but of course her dad was busy with other things. A message finally arrived at the end of her last class and it was all Zoe could do not to squeal when she read that Koko had reached Tanglewood safely.

"She's here!" Zoe said when she found Oliver in the after-school crowd.

Oliver grinned, his eyes gleaming. "I know. Dad messaged me – he says her roar is even louder that Tindu's."

The journey home seemed to take forever, although Zoe and Oliver talked non-stop about Koko the entire time. They raced back from the bus stop, arranging to meet at the tiger enclosure as soon as they'd changed out of their school uniforms.

"I hope she's out of her traveling crate," Zoe said, as she hurried along the path to the manor house. "Do you think she'll be much smaller than Tindu?"

"Probably. But if her roar is anything to go by then it sounds like she can hold her own," Oliver said, heading off towards Magpie Cottage. "See you in a minute – last one there is the tigers' treat."

Max, Cassie and Zoe's dad were at the tiger enclosure when Zoe arrived. She glanced over her shoulder, looking for Oliver, and saw him running towards her. She hid a little smile of satisfaction at having beaten him – just because they were friends didn't mean they couldn't compete sometimes.

"Hello, you two," Cassie said, as Oliver puffed up. "I thought it wouldn't be long before you appeared."

"How's Koko?" Zoe asked breathlessly. "Did she have a good journey?"

"She did," Max said. "And she's nowhere near as timid as Tindu was. She's out of the crate already."

Right on cue, a deep roar filled the air. Zoe felt a thrill of excitement – the sound might even be louder than Sinbad! "So where is she? Can we see her?"

Her dad smiled. "We're keeping her inside for now. Tindu is prowling around the outdoor enclosure. He knows there's something going on."

"Hasn't he seen her?" Oliver asked.

Cassie shook her head. "We're keeping them apart for now, although they'll be able to see each other through the wire once we bring Tindu into the den for the night."

Mr. Fox opened the door to the den. "You know the drill. You'll have to be very quiet and stand back, with no sudden—"

"Movements or noises," Zoe and Oliver chorused together.

They grinned at each other.

"We know, Dad," Zoe said. "We'll be quiet, okay?"

There were three parts to the den, each separated by bars. The one on the right-hand side was where Tindu usually slept, Koko was occupying the area on the left, and the middle space was empty to allow the tigers to see each other without being able to touch. The female tiger was smaller than Tindu, but she had the same amber eyes and breathtaking fur. Her whiskers were longer and her paws seemed slightly more delicate than Tindu's. Zoe wasn't surprised to see her pacing back and forth the way Tindu had when he'd first arrived, but she was surprised by Koko's attitude. She behaved as though she owned the place already, letting out a low rumbling growl of dissatisfaction at being trapped inside the den. She padded over to the hatch and let out a roar that made the hair on the back of Zoe's neck stand on end. She stepped back with a gasp.

"I think she wants to go outside," Max said, wiggling his fingers in his ears.

Zoe watched in electrified amazement as the tiger prowled. Koko might be smaller than Tindu but she had no problem making herself heard. Her dad was right, Zoe thought with a grin: Koko *was* going to run circles around Tindu when they met!

Chapter Eleven

Once all the park visitors had left, Cassie and Mr. Fox agreed it was time to bring Tindu into the den.

"We don't know how they're going to react to each other," Mr. Fox warned Zoe and Oliver, handing each of them a pair of earplugs. "Things could get pretty loud and bad-tempered."

"Judging from the way Koko behaved earlier, I think that's a definite possibility," Oliver muttered to Zoe as they put the earplugs in.

Everything became slightly muffled then, although Zoe could still hear Koko's grumbles as she paced. Cassie pulled open the hatch on Tindu's side and they waited. Only a few minutes passed before his whiskery muzzle appeared in the gap, but he wasn't more than a few steps in when he caught sight of Koko and froze.

His jowls drew back in a snarl and a low growl escaped him. Koko had spotted him too and had stopped pacing to glare at him. Slowly, Tindu moved forwards, his eyes fixed on the other tiger. He snarled again and pressed his nose against the bars.

Koko was watching Tindu just as closely. She patrolled the bars closest to him, never taking her eyes from his, growling and rumbling constantly. Her tail swished from side to side, reminding Zoe very much of the way Lucky behaved when she was unhappy in her cage back at the medical center. And then Koko bared her teeth and let out a thunderous roar. Tindu responded with a snarling roar of his own, making Zoe very glad she had her earplugs. The roaring didn't last long, however, and the two tigers settled into a curious but mistrustful pacing, each watching the other carefully.

"I think we should leave them to it," Cassie said, removing her earplugs. "They can't hurt each other and maybe by the morning they'll be more settled."

The adults huddled together, clearly discussing the tigers. It didn't sound as though anything more would happen that night, so Zoe and Oliver waved goodbye and set off home.

"I'm glad I don't have to sleep next door to those two tonight," Zoe said as they made their way out of the park. "I don't think anyone nearby is going to get much sleep."

"Maybe they'll make friends overnight," Oliver said. "You never know, they might get along really well once they stop trying to prove who's boss."

Zoe grinned. That was exactly what had happened between her and Oliver when they first met. It was only when they'd been forced to work together to find the lost baby zebra, Flash, that they'd finally become friends.

"Maybe," she said. "Although I get the feeling that Koko is always going to be the one in charge."

Oliver shrugged. "Maybe. I just want them to like each other – the world needs more Sumatran tigers."

"That's true," Zoe agreed. "It would be amazing if they had some cubs. How cute would they be?"

Oliver laughed. "I think they need to stop acting as though they want to bite chunks out of each other first."

"Good point," Zoe said. "Should I ask my dad if we can go and see them before school tomorrow?"

"Okay," Oliver said. "Message me once you know."

Zoe waved goodbye and headed towards the medical center. She wanted to snatch a quick visit with Lucky before settling down to her homework. She spent a few minutes tossing the kitten's ball around, giggling when Lucky lay on her back and waved all four paws in the air to catch it.

She mewed pitifully when Zoe closed her cage, making her heart ache for the lonely little tabby. It really didn't seem fair that the cat had to stay locked away on her own, especially when she was so friendly, but Zoe understood that the welfare of Tindu and Koko and all the other Tanglewood cats had to come first.

"Never mind, Lucky," she called as she left. "One day soon we'll find you someone to purr with."

As Zoe headed for home she heard another ear-splitting roar echoing through the early evening gloom. *Is that Tindu or Koko?* she wondered, before deciding it was impossible to tell. She imagined the two of them locked in their dens, growling and staring at each other, and hoped they'd be friends by the morning.

There was good news when Zoe hurried down to Tanglewood HQ before breakfast on Thursday morning: Koko and Tindu seemed to have settled down during the night.

The bad news was that they now seemed to be completely ignoring each other.

"It will have all changed again by the time you get home from school," Ruth the security guard said. "You mark my words – I've spent a lot of time watching animals and their moods change faster than the weather."

And she was right. Zoe and Oliver went straight to the tiger enclosure after school and discovered both tigers were outside. They were separated by a tall wire fence down the center of the habitat; every now and then one of them would peer through the metal as though planning how to invade. But at least the roaring competition had stopped.

"Koko has settled in fast," Zoe said to her dad, who was observing the tigers and making notes.

He nodded. "She's a lot more confident than Tindu. Cassie says she's eaten this morning, too. The main problem now is whether she and Tindu accept each other. If they don't, we won't be able to breed them and Koko will probably have to move to another zoo."

Zoe's tummy lurched. "I don't want her to go."

Dad sighed. "I don't either, but there are so few Sumatran tigers left that we can't afford to keep two together when they don't get along."

Zoe felt even more anxious. If Tindu and Koko didn't like each other, Koko would have to leave and the breeding program all over the country would need to change.

"Please make friends," she whispered, watching Koko prowl along the fence that separated her from Tindu. "If Oliver and I can do it, so can you!"

Now that Koko had arrived, preparation for the Terrific Tigers weekend exploded into a frenzy. With only one day left to put plans in place, Zoe's mom had been on the phone with all the local newspapers and Dad had called in a favor with a celebrity tiger expert to come and give a talk. There was even a rumor about a TV news channel joining them to film the tigers.

The pressure for Tindu and Koko to get along was enormous. Zoe was sure the animals must be able to feel the tension in the air, although Cassie and the other keepers were doing their best to make sure it was business as usual around the park.

"They don't seem to hate each other," Zoe's mom said, as they discussed Tindu and Koko at breakfast time on Friday.

"But they don't appear to be interested in each other, either," Dad said, sighing. "It's so hard to tell how they'll react when they meet face to face, and the last thing we need is a full-on tiger fight."

"Samuel and Michael had a fight at preschool yesterday," Rory said solemnly. "Miss Peters said they had to think about what they'd done."

Zoe smiled. "I think tigers are a little more difficult."

"But we're running out of time," Mom said. "Terrific Tigers is our chance to show them off and raise some funds for tiger conservation all over the world. It would be much better if they were on display together, rather than separated by a wire fence."

"Maybe you should just give them a chance," Zoe said, deep in thought. "Oliver and I almost hated each other until we had to work together."

Her mom laughed. "That's true. We thought you'd never be friends."

"I don't know," Dad said, rubbing his chin. "We don't want to rush this."

"We could do it in the den so it's easier to control them," Mom suggested. "Have the hoses on stand-by in case we need to split them up."

Dad frowned thoughtfully. "I've used fire extinguishers to stop animals from fighting before. The noise is enough to scare them."

"Well then," Mom said. "We'll never know unless we try."

Dad nodded. "Okay. I'll speak to Cassie and arrange something for this evening, once the park has closed."

Zoe opened her mouth to speak but Dad beat her to it. "I know – you and Oliver want to be there."

She held her breath, nodding hopefully.

"Okay," Dad sighed. "But if the tigers get too bad-tempered, you'll need to be ready to leave so you don't get in the way. Agreed?"

"Agreed," Zoe said quickly and gulped down the rest of her food. She couldn't wait to go and give Oliver the good news!

Zoe felt as though the school day would never end – it felt like years until the bell rang at the end of the day. At home, Zoe got changed as fast as she could and raced through her jobs in the park.

Lucky watched her with big eyes as she hurriedly changed the water and cleaned out the litter box.

"Sorry, kitty," she said, giving the cat a quick pat. "No time to play today!"

The sun was starting to set but the temperature inside the tiger house was still warm. Zoe thought she'd have been sweating even if it had been a cold day. So much rested on whether Tindu and Koko got along. She could almost taste the tension in the air.

Cassie and Oliver were both there, along with Max and both of Zoe's parents. Rory was being babysat by Dolly, the catering manager. A couple of other keepers, Mizbah and Nick, stood as close to the outer bars as possible, each holding a water hose in case a fight broke out between the tigers. Max was waiting beside one of the pulleys that opened the hatches.

Tindu was in the den to the right and Koko was on the left. The area in the center was empty, as always. Cassie cast a nervous glance at Mizbah and Nick. "Ready?"

They nodded. Zoe looked at her father, poised with the fire extinguisher, ready to let it off into the air if the tigers became aggressive. He lifted a hand and gave a little wave. "I'm ready and waiting too. Over to you, Cassie."

Taking a deep breath, the big-cat keeper pulled the mechanism that opened the hatch between

Tindu and the center space. Tindu's head swung around and he padded forwards to investigate. Cassie nodded to Max on the other side of the room and he raised the hatch between Koko and the middle. Koko stopped pacing and let out a soft growl.

Zoe clenched her fists, her heart thumping. This was it – make or break time. She risked a quick look at Oliver – his face was pale and anxious.

Tindu slunk through the gap, his eyes fixed on Koko. He opened his mouth and a long rumble filled the air. Then Koko seemed to realize she could reach him and dipped her head through the gap on her side. They stayed like that for a moment, fangs bared, snarling at each other, and Zoe thought her heart might thud right out of her chest.

"Be ready with the hoses," her father murmured. "Any minute now."

Koko edged forwards. The snarling intensified. Tindu came all the way inside the middle den and the two tigers began to circle, their eyes locked and their bodies close to the ground. Zoe almost couldn't bear to watch – it felt like one of them had to pounce. What if they hurt each other? What if the water hoses didn't break them up?

The breath caught in Zoe's throat as Koko stopped pacing and took a step towards Tindu. She put her nose right up against his and let out a funny snorting snuffle. Tindu jerked his head away and Koko repeated the noise, blowing right into his face. Zoe felt all the tension whoosh out of her. She recognized that sound! It was the sound Tindu had made when he'd wanted to show Cassie they were friends. It was a chuffle.

"Good girl, Koko," Cassie murmured. "Now go on, Tindu. It's your turn."

For a moment, Zoe thought Tindu was going to ignore Koko's gesture of friendship. But then he butted his nose gently against hers and snorted a chuffle of his own.

Mr. Fox lowered the fire extinguisher to the ground. "Thank goodness for that. I don't think we're going to need this now."

Zoe beamed at the tigers, who were gently sniffing each other and yowling in greeting. "Well done, guys. Just in time for your big day tomorrow!"

Chapter Twelve

Saturday morning dawned bright and clear. Zoe woke early, her stomach fizzing with nerves and excitement. Grabbing a banana for breakfast, she dashed over to Tanglewood HQ to observe the tigers.

"How are they looking?" she asked Hans.

He pointed to the screen. "See for yourself."

Zoe looked anxiously at the wall of monitors, but she needn't have worried – Tindu and Koko were sitting side by side on one of the high platforms, sunbathing together as though they had been friends for years.

"They've been like that for about an hour," Hans explained. "And before that, they were watching the workmen take down the wooden fences from around the outside of the enclosure – they were very curious about that."

Zoe peered at the screen – now that Hans mentioned it, she could see that the boards were gone. "Great," she said, smiling. "I can't wait for our visitors to see how incredible Tindu and Koko are too."

She watched the tigers doze in the sun for a little while longer, then headed into the park to see how she could help. With a little luck, major crowds would be on their way to Tanglewood so it was important that the animals and their enclosures looked their best. But first she took a detour via the medical center. Lucky wouldn't be on display, but she needed Zoe's time and attention too.

Lucky wound herself around Zoe's feet, purring,

as she changed the cat's food and water.

"I'm sorry you're stuck in here while everyone else is out having fun," Zoe told the cat, trying not to feel guilty as she lifted her back into her pen.

Lucky let out a mournful meow. Zoe sighed and rubbed her ears. "As soon as this weekend is out of the way, we'll start looking for a new home for you." She blinked and swallowed hard. "A forever home this time."

Over at Guinea Pig Central, Zoe did a quick clean up and then hurried across to check on Flash. He came trotting over when he saw Zoe, braying in greeting. Zoe laughed.

"I hope you're ready for some big crowds today," she said, feeding him a carrot top she'd brought especially for him. "They might come for the tigers but I bet they'll fall in love with you!"

Next, she headed over to the meerkats. Their keeper, Jack, was already there, giving the furry little creatures their breakfast.

"Big day today, guys," she called to them as they

munched on their fruit and vegetables. "Be on your best behavior!"

Everywhere she looked, Zoe saw keepers rushing around to make sure everything was ready. Just after nine o'clock, the TV news crew arrived and began to set up. Then the press arrived and Zoe's dad gave them a quick tour. And at nine-thirty on the dot, the gates opened and Tanglewood's Terrific Tigers weekend officially began.

People crowded around Tindu and Koko's enclosure, chattering with excitement. Cassie had given the tigers some large cardboard boxes to play with and they were making everyone laugh by jumping in and out of them as though they were kittens.

"Look at that – even big cats can't resist a box," Zoe heard one woman say to another.

"They look like they've been friends for life," the other woman said. "Are they brother and sister?"

"No," Zoe said, smiling. "They're not related. In fact, we're hoping they'll have some cubs in the future."

The women looked at her in delight. "Now that would definitely be worth coming back for!"

Just then, Zoe heard someone calling her. She turned around to see Mom heading her way, with her aunt and little brother at her side.

"Auntie Nina!" Zoe cried, running to give her aunt a huge hug. "I didn't know you were coming today!"

"I wanted to surprise you," Auntie Nina said, smiling. Then she looked past Zoe, to Tindu and Koko, who were still playing with the boxes.

"Look at those two," she said, laughing. "What on earth did cats do for fun before humans invented cardboard?"

"Speaking of cats," Mom said, clearing her throat. "We have some good news. But I'll let Auntie Nina tell you."

Auntie Nina dragged her gaze away from the tigers. "I hear you found a stray cat and have been looking for its owner."

Zoe nodded. "That's right. I wanted to keep her

but Dad says she can't stay at Tanglewood in case she makes the big cats sick, so I'm going to start looking for a new home for her on Monday."

Auntie Nina's eyes twinkled. "How would you like it if she came to stay with me for a little while? Just until Max is sure she's not carrying any diseases?"

Zoe stared at her doubtfully. "That would be great, but Lucky deserves a permanent home."

Mom put her arm around Zoe's shoulders. "Dad and I have been very impressed by the way you've helped us since we moved into Tanglewood. We agree that it's time you had a pet of your own. So as long as Max is certain Lucky is healthy, then she'll be able to come back here to live in a few months' time."

Auntie Nina smiled. "And if she isn't as healthy as we'd like, she can live with me forever. You'll still be able to see her without worrying that she'll infect the other cats then – how does that sound?"

Zoe's eyes widened and she thought she might burst from happiness. "Are you kidding?" she exploded in delight. "That would be amazing. Thank you!"

She flung her arms out and gathered her mom and her aunt into a squashy group hug. "This is the best day ever!"

"It's not over yet," Dad said, coming to join in with the hug. "I've just checked our ticket sales and today is our busiest day ever. Pre-orders for tomorrow look amazing too."

Zoe beamed in delight. "Awesome!"

"Zoe!" Oliver called, racing towards her. "You have got to come and see this! Tindu and Koko, they're—"

"They're what?" she demanded, feeling her stomach swoop with fear. What if the tigers had decided they weren't friends after all?

Grinning, Oliver shook his head. "Just come and see!"

Zoe's whole family followed as he led them towards the tiger house. There was a huge crowd – people were laughing and pointing and some were even standing on the picnic tables to get a better view. The air was filled by the click of cameras and phones as visitors snapped photos.

"What's going on?" Zoe asked in bewilderment. "What are Tindu and Koko doing?"

Oliver pulled her arm and led her to a gap in the crowd so that she could see. And almost immediately, Zoe started to laugh. Tindu and Koko were splashing around in their pool, batting the big red tiger ball back and forth between them! As she watched, Tindu rose up on his hind legs, water dripping from his whiskers and fur, and pounced onto the ball. More water splashed into the air, catching Koko squarely in the face. She shook her head and bounded towards the ball. Opening her jaws wide, she wrapped her teeth around it and carried it away, much to Tindu's disappointment. Koko took the ball underneath one of the platforms and began to gnaw at it.

"Poor Tindu," Zoe said, as the crowd let out a loud *awww.*

"Don't worry about him," Oliver said, pointing at Tindu, who was creeping towards Koko as though he was stalking a gazelle. "I think Koko is about to get a big surprise."

Seconds later, Tindu pounced, knocking the ball away from Koko. She growled in mock temper and began to chase him around the enclosure. The crowd laughed and cheered, and Zoe couldn't help giggling too.

"I might be biased but I think our tigers are pretty terrific," she said, smiling at Oliver.

He grinned back and held up his hand. "They are. High five for Tindu and Koko!"

Zoe slapped her hand against his. "And high five for Tanglewood – the best animal park in the world!"

The End

Everybody's Talking About
TANGLEWOOD ANIMAL PARK!

"This is a roarsome book! I love it! 1,000 out of 10!" Finley ☺, age 8

"Outstandingly gripping"
Daniel, age 8

"I did not want to put it down because I did not want the fun to end."
Dior, age 8

"I love reading about all of the animals. The book makes me want to go and visit Tanglewood."
Freya, age 6

"I really loved reading this book. 10/10." Holly, age 9

"I just could not take my eyes off this book. It reminds me so much about myself and my love for animals, just like Zoe!"
Lila, age 10

"I think this book is the best book I have ever read." Ava, age 6

Ridha, age 8

"I'd love to live with the main character Zoe. I will be telling all my friends to read this book."
Charlotte, age 9

"When I read about Flash the zebra being born it made me feel emotional."
Leila, age 8

"This book was amazingly cool!!!"

"I wish I lived in Tanglewood like Zoe. This book was amazingly cool!!!"

Meet
Tamsyn Murray,
author of
TANGLEWOOD
ANIMAL PARK!

Where did you get the idea for Tanglewood Animal Park? Anyone who knows me will tell you I'm animal crazy! I'm also lucky enough to live very close to an amazing wildlife park and I visit it a lot. One day I started thinking about how great it would be to have a zoo of my own and – BOOM! – Tanglewood was born!

If you could be any animal, what would you be? I think I'd quite like to be a red panda. They always seem very contented and chilled out when I see them at my local animal park. They're cute and cuddly, too, and can sleep way up high in the trees.

Of course I wouldn't mind being a tiger, although I'd spend all day looking at my reflection!

Oh, this is a tough question. You're sure I can only choose one? Hmm... I think it would probably be one of the big cats; snow leopards or perhaps tigers. I'm fascinated by the pattern on the snow leopards' fur, and by their super-long, furry tails. But I also love the tigers' stripes and the tufty little white spots at the very tip of their ears. I wouldn't be able to resist stroking them, though, so maybe it's better that I'm not a big-cat keeper!

I couldn't possibly choose! *Black Beauty* by Anna Sewell, told entirely by the horse, is a classic. There was a series called *The Animals of Farthing Wood* about animals journeying in search of a new home which was HUGE when I was younger. But if you really made me choose, I'd have to go for *The Diary of a Killer Cat* by Anne Fine, because Tuffy and his adventures still make me laugh now.

Usborne Quicklinks

For links to websites where you can watch video clips about lots of different animals, find out about the life of zookeepers and test your animal know-how with quizzes, games and activities, go to the Usborne Quicklinks website at www.usborne.com/quicklinks and enter the keywords "Troublesome Tiger."

When using the internet, please make sure you follow our three basic rules:
• Always ask an adult's permission before using the internet.
• Never give out personal information, such as your name, address, the name of your school or telephone number.
• If a website asks you to type in your name or email address, check with an adult first.

To find out more about internet safety, go to the Help and advice page at the Usborne Quicklinks website. We recommend that children are supervised while using the internet.